"It's Imperative That I Marry A Woman Who'll Make A Good Princess. I Know My Requirements."

"Your requirements?" Wasn't that just like him.

"For pity's sake, Adam. You do need help."

"Not with my list or what's on it. That's non-negotiable. I just need help with being a better me and a much better date."

She shook her head. "You don't need help being a better you. You just have to let people see the real you, not the you you think you have to be."

A wry smile touched his lips. "So you'll help me?"

Had she just put her foot into a trap that was starting to close?

* * *

To find out more about Harlequin Desire's upcoming books and to chat with authors and editors, become a fan of Harlequin Desire on Facebook, www.facebook.com/HarlequinDesire, or follow us on Twitter, www.twitter.com/desireeditors!

Dear Reader,

When I started writing this book, I thought it would be all about my heroine, Danni, teaching Adam, the somewhat reserved hero (he is a prince after all, so he is allowed to be a little reserved) to lighten up and have more fun. She did that, but what I enjoyed during the process was discovering that Adam had a lot to teach Danni, too. They weren't as dissimilar as she (and I) had first thought.

I hope you enjoy their journey.

Warmest wishes,

Sandra

SANDRA HYATT

LESSONS IN SEDUCTION

Harlequin®

Desire

Recycling programs
for this product may
not exist in your area.

ISBN-13: 978-0-373-73141-1

LESSONS IN SEDUCTION

SANDRA HYATT

After completing a business degree, traveling and then settling into a career in marketing, Sandra Hyatt was relieved to experience one of life's eureka! moments while on maternity leave—she discovered that writing books, although a lot slower, was just as much fun as reading them.

She knows life doesn't always hand out happy endings and figures that's why books ought to. She loves being along for the journey with her characters as they work around, over and through the obstacles standing in their way.

Sandra has lived in both the U.S. and England and currently lives near the coast in New Zealand with her high school sweetheart and their two children.

You can visit her at www.sandrahyatt.com.

To Gaynor and Allan.

One

Keep calm and carry on. Danni St. Claire had seen the slogan somewhere and it seemed apt. She flexed her gloved fingers before tightening them again around the steering wheel.

Her passengers, one in particular, behind the privacy partition, would pay her no attention. They so seldom did. Especially if she just did her job and did it well. In this case, that job entailed getting Adam Marconi, heir to the throne of the European principality of San Philippe, and his glamorous date for the evening, back to their respective destinations.

Without incident.

And most importantly without Adam realizing that she was driving for him. She could do that. Especially if she kept her mouth shut. Occasionally she had trouble in that department, speaking when either her timing or her words weren't appropriate or required. But she could do it tonight. How hard could it be? She'd have no cause to speak. Someone else would be responsible for opening and closing the door for him. All she had to do was drive. Which, if she did it well meant without calling attention to herself. She would be invisible. A shadow. At a stop light she pulled her father's chauffeur's cap a little lower on her forehead.

A job of a sensitive nature, the palace had said. And so she'd known her father, although he'd never admit it, would rather the job didn't go to Wrightson, the man he saw as a rival for his position as head driver. Danni still had clearance from when she'd driven for the palace before, back when she was putting herself through college. She hadn't seen Adam since that last time.

All the same she hadn't known it would be Adam she'd be driving for tonight. When she'd intercepted the call, she'd thought all she'd have to do was pick up Adam's date for the evening, a beautiful, elegant Fulbright scholar, and take her to the restaurant. But then, and she should have realized there'd be a "then" because such instructions usually came on a need-to-know basis, she had to drive them both home. It was obvious, with hindsight, that there would be something that justified the sensitivity required.

Her stomach growled. She hadn't had time for her own dinner. And her father never saw the need to keep a wee stash of food in the glove compartment. There'd be all sorts of gourmet delicacies in the discreet fridge in the back but she could hardly ask them to pass her something over. Not appropriate at the best of times. Even less so tonight. She'd had to make do with crunch-

ing her way through the roll of breath mints she kept
in her pocket.

At a set of lights she glanced in the rearview mirror
and rolled her eyes. If the palace had thought that sensitivity was required because there might be shenanigans
in the backseat, they needn't have worried. Adam and
his date were deep in conversation; both looked utterly
serious, as though they were solving the problems of the
world. Maybe they were. Maybe that was what princes
and scholars did on dates. And Danni should probably
be grateful that someone had more on their mind than
what they were going to be able to unearth for dinner
from the shelves of the fridge.

Still, she would have thought the point of the date
was to get to know one another. Not to solve the problems of the world, not to discuss topics with such utter
earnestness that they looked like two members of the
supreme court about to hand down a judgment. Danni
sighed. Who was she to know about royal protocol?
Things were different in Adam's world. They always
had been. Even as a teen he'd seemed to carry the
weight of the world on his shoulders. Had taken his
responsibilities and his duties seriously. Too seriously,
she'd thought.

What she did know was that Adam was on the lookout for a suitable wife.

And one of the prospective candidates was in the
backseat with him.

At thirty-one years old, he was expected—by his
father and by the country, if the media were to be be-
lieved—to do the right thing. The right thing meant
getting married, settling down and providing heirs,

preferably male, to continue the Marconi line and to ensure succession.

If anyone had cared to ask Danni, she'd have happily shared her opinion that what the prince needed was to shake things up a little, not to settle down. She'd always thought the narrow focus of his life stopped him from seeing what was really there—the variety and opportunities. And for as long as he kept that narrow focus, it stopped anyone else from seeing who he could be, if he only let himself.

For Adam, finding the right woman meant dating. Romantic dinners like the one she'd just picked him up from in the revolving restaurant that towered above the new part of the city.

Maybe, instead of dwelling on Adam, Danni should be trying to pick up a few pointers on how a real woman comported herself on a date. She glanced in the back. Obviously sitting up straight was important, manicured hands folded demurely in the lap, polite smiles, what looked like polite laughter, occasional fluttering of long dark eyelashes, a slight tilt to the head exposing a pale slender neck.

Who was she kidding? Danni didn't do fluttering. And manicuring with the life she led—working in the motor-racing industry—was a waste of time and money.

She might sometimes wish she wasn't seen quite so much as one of the boys by all her male colleagues, but she knew she couldn't go so far as to look and behave like a Barbie clone. Scratch that, even Barbie had more personality than the woman in the backseat seemed to. Didn't they make a Pilot Barbie and NASCAR Barbie? Although she'd never heard of a Speak-Your-Mind Barbie or a Put-Your-Foot-In-Your-Mouth Barbie. Danni

mentally pulled herself up. She was taking out her inse-
curities and inadequacies on a woman she didn't even
know.

She glanced up, again determined to think better of
the couple in the backseat. No. Surely not? But yes, a
second glance confirmed that Adam did indeed have
his laptop out, and that both he and his date were point-
ing at something on the screen.

"Way to romance a woman, Adam," she muttered.

He couldn't possibly have heard, not with the privacy screen up and her speaker off, but Adam glanced
up, and for a fraction of a second his gaze brushed over
hers in the mirror. Danni bit her tongue. Hard. Fortunately there was no flicker of recognition in his dark
eyes. His gaze didn't pause; it swept over hers as if she
was invisible, or of no more importance than the back
of her headrest. That was good. If only she could trust
in it.

Because she wasn't supposed to be driving for him.

Because he'd banned her. Actually, it wasn't an official ban. He'd only intimated that he no longer wanted
her to drive for him. But in palace circles an intimation
by Adam was as good as a ban. Nothing official was
necessary.

Though, honestly, no reasonable person would blame
her for the coffee incident. The pothole had been un-
avoidable. She sighed. It wasn't like she needed the job
then or now. Then she'd had her studies to pursue and
now she had her career as part of the team bringing a
Grand Prix to San Philippe.

But, she reminded herself, her father did need the
job. For his sense of self and his purpose in life, if not
for the money. Close to retirement age, he'd begun to

live in fear of being replaced in the job that gave his life meaning. The job that his father and his father's father before him had held.

Danni didn't look in the mirror again, not into the backseat anyway. She consoled herself with the fact that her unofficial banning had been five years ago while driving on her summer break, and surely Adam, with far more important things to think about, would have forgotten it. And definitely have forgiven her. In those intervening years he'd become a stranger to her. So she drove, taking no shortcuts, to San Philippe's premier hotel and eased to a stop beneath the portico.

"Wait here." Adam's deep voice, so used to command, sounded through the speaker system.

A hotel valet opened the rear door, and Adam and the perfectly elegant Ms. Fulbright Scholar with the endless legs exited. Clara. That was her name.

Wait here could mean anything from thirty seconds to thirty minutes, to hours—she'd had it happen before with other passengers. He was seeing a woman home from a date; Danni had no idea if it was their first or second or something more. Maybe Clara would invite him in. Maybe she'd slide his tie undone and tear that stuffy suit jacket off his broad shoulders and drag him into her hotel room, her lips locked on his, making him stop thinking and start feeling, her fingers threading into his dark hair, dropping to explore his perfectly honed chest. Whoa. Danni put the brakes on her thought processes hearing the mental screech that was in part a protest at just how quickly her mind had gone down that track and just how vividly it had provided the images of a shirtless Adam.

Danni had grown up on the palace estates, so yes,

despite their five-year age difference they'd sometimes played together, as had all the children living on the palace grounds. There was a time when she'd thought of him as almost a friend. Certainly as her ally and some-time protector. So she couldn't entirely see him as just a royal, but he would be Crown Prince one day. And she *knew* she wasn't supposed to imagine the Crown Prince shirtless. She also knew that she could too easily have gone further still with her imaginings.

Besides, Danni hadn't picked up any of those types of signals from the couple in the back, but then again, what did she know. Maybe well brought up, cultured people did things differently. Maybe they were better at hiding their simmering passions.

She eased lower in her seat, cranked up the stereo and pulled down the brim of her cap over her eyes to block out all the light from the hotel. The good thing about driving for the royal family was that at least she wouldn't be told to move on.

She leapt up again when she felt and heard the rear door open. "Holy—"

Minutes. He'd only been minutes. She jabbed at the stereo's off button. The sound faded as Adam slid back into the car.

Utterly unruffled. Not so much as a mismatched button, a hair out of place, or even a lipstick smudge. No flush to his skin. He looked every bit as serious as before as he leaned back in his seat. Nothing soft or softened about him. Even the bump on his nose that should have detracted from the perfection of his face somehow added to it. Or maybe that was just wishful thinking.

Had they even kissed?

Danni shook her head and eased away from the hotel. She shouldn't care. She didn't care.

Normally, with any other passenger she'd say something. Just a "Pleasant evening, sir?" At times a chauffeur served as a sort of butler on wheels. But Adam wasn't any other passenger, and with his head tipped back and his eyes closed, he clearly wasn't needing conversation from her. Long may the silence last. She'd have him back to the palace in fifteen minutes. Then she'd be free. She'd have pulled it off. Without incident. Her father would be back tomorrow. No one would be any the wiser.

Finally, a quarter of an hour later, she flexed her fingers as the second set of palace gates eased open. Minutes later, she drew to a sedate stop in front of the entrance to Adam's wing, the wheels crunching quietly on the gravel. Nobody knew what it cost her, the restraint she exercised, in never once skidding to a stop or better yet finishing with a perfectly executed handbrake slide, lining up the rear door precisely with the entrance. But she could imagine it. The advanced security and high-performance modules of her training had been her favorite parts.

Her smile dimmed when the valet who ought to be opening the door failed to materialize. Too late, Danni remembered her father complaining about Adam dispensing with that tradition at his private residence. Her father had been as appalled as if Adam had decided to stop wearing shoes in public. Danni didn't have a problem with it. Except for now. Now, Adam could hardly open his own door while he was asleep.

There was nothing else for it. She got out, walked around the back of the car and after a quick scan of the surroundings opened Adam's door then stood to the side, facing away from him. She'd hoped the fact that the car had stopped and the noise and motion, albeit slight, of the door being opened would wake him. When he didn't appear after a few seconds she turned and bent to look into the car.

Her heart gave a peculiar flip. Adam's eyes were still closed and finally his face and his mouth had softened, looking not at all serious and unreachable. Looking instead lush and sensuous. And really, he had unfairly gorgeous eyelashes—thick and dark. And he smelled divine. She almost wanted to lean in closer, to inhale more deeply.

"Adam," she said quietly. Right now she'd have been more comfortable with "sir" or "your highness" because she suddenly felt the need for the appropriate distance and formality, to stop her from thinking inappropriate and way too informal thoughts of the heir apparent. To stop her from wanting to touch that small bump on the bridge of his nose. But one of the things Adam had always insisted on was that the personal staff, particularly the ones who'd effectively grown up with him in the palace circles, use his name.

He was trying to be a prince of the times. Secretly she thought he might have been happier and more comfortable a century or two ago.

"Adam." She tried to speak a little louder but her voice came out as a hoarse whisper. Danni swallowed. All she had to do was wake him and then back out of the car. She leaned closer, steeling herself to try again. Ordering her voice to be normal. It was only Adam after all. She'd known him most of her life though five years and infinite degrees in rank separated them.

His eyes flew open. His gaze locked on hers and for a second, darkened. Not a hint of lethargy there. Danni's mouth ran suddenly dry. "Can I help you?" he asked, his voice low and silky with a hint of mockery as though he knew she'd been staring. Fascinated.

Disconcerted by the intimacy she'd imagined in his gaze, she responded with an unfamiliar heat quivering through her. "Yes. You can help me by waking up and getting out of my car."

"Your car, Danielle?" He lifted one eyebrow.

"Your car. But I'm the one who still needs to drive it round to the garage," she snapped. Oops. Definitely not supposed to snap at the prince, no matter how shocked at herself she was. Definitely not appropriate. But her curt response seemed almost to please him because the corners of his lips twitched. And then, too soon, flattened again.

Danni swallowed. She needed to backpedal. Fast. "We've reached the palace. I trust you had a pleasant evening." She used her blandest voice as she backed out of the car. Stick to the script. That was all she had to do.

Adam followed her and stood, towering over her, his gaze contemplative. "Very. Thank you."

"Really?" She winced. That so was not in the script. What had happened to her resolve to be a shadow?

His gaze narrowed, changing from contemplative to enquiring with a hint of accusation. "You doubt me, Danielle?" A cold breeze wrapped around her.

Well, yes. But she could hardly say that and she oughtn't to lie. She searched for a way around it. "No one would know other than yourself."

"No, they wouldn't."

She willed him to just step away from the car. Go on into the palace. Get on with saving the nation and the world. Then she could close the door and drive away and get something to eat. And it would be as if tonight had never happened. There would be no repercussions. Not for her and not for her father.

But he didn't move. He stood absolutely still. Her stomach rumbled into the silence.

"You haven't eaten?"

"I'm fine."

Again the silence. Awkward and strained. If he would just go.

He stood still. Watching her. "I didn't realize you were driving for us again. I thought you were in the States."

"I was for a while. I came back." Three-and-a-half years ago she had moved back for good. "But this is temporary, just for tonight in fact. I'm staying with Dad and he had something come up." Danni held her breath. Did he remember the ban? Would it matter now?

He nodded and she let out her breath. "Everything's all right with him?"

"Absolutely. A sick friend. He'll be back tomorrow."

"Good." Adam turned to go into the palace and then just when she thought she was free, turned back. "What was it you said?"

"He'll be back tomorrow."

"Not then. Earlier. When you were driving."

All manner of desperate, inappropriate words raced through her mind. No, no, no. He couldn't have heard.

"I can't remember." So much for her principles. She was lying through her teeth.

"It was around the time I got the laptop out to show

Clara the geographic distribution of lava from the 1300 eruption of Ducal Island."

She did roll her eyes then; she couldn't help it. He was too much. "My point exactly," she said, throwing her hand up in surrender. "I said, 'Way to romance a woman, Adam.' Really. The geographic distribution of lava?"

His expression went cold.

There was a line somewhere in the receding distance, one she'd long since stepped over. Her only hope was to make him see the truth of her assertions. "Come on, Adam. You weren't always this stuffy." She'd known him when he was still a boy becoming a man. And later she'd occasionally seen glimpses of an altogether different man beneath the surface when he'd forgotten, however briefly, who he was supposed to be and just allowed himself to act naturally.

Now wasn't that time.

His brows shot up. But Danni couldn't stop herself.

"What woman wants to talk about lava and rock formations on a date?" Too late, Danni remembered the saying about how when you found yourself in a hole the best course of action was to stop digging.

The brows, dark and heavy, drew together. "Clara is a Fulbright scholar. She studied geology. She was interested."

"Maybe she was. But surely she can read a textbook for that kind of thing. It's great if you're planning a lecture tour together but it's hardly romantic. Where's the poetry, the magic, in that? You weren't even looking into her eyes, you were looking at the screen. And did you even kiss her when you escorted her to her door?"

"I'm not sure that's any of your business, but yes."
Somehow he'd made himself taller.

She wasn't going to be intimidated. "Some kiss,
huh?"

"And you'd be an expert on kissing and on romance?
What would you suggest? Discussing the specifications
of the Bentley perhaps?"

Danni took a little step back as though that could
distance her from the stab of hurt. She liked cars. She
couldn't help that. Wouldn't want to, even if Adam, who
she knew for a fact also liked cars, considered it a failing in a woman. "No. I'm not an expert on romance.
But I am a woman."

"You're sure about that?"

This time she didn't even try to hide her mortification. She took a much bigger step back. Her heart
thumped, seeming to echo in her chest. She clamped
shut the jaw that had fallen open.

Her uniform—a dark jacket and pants—had been
designed for men and adapted for her, the only female
driver. It was well tailored but it wasn't exactly feminine. It wasn't supposed to be. And it was nothing like
Clara's soft pink dress that had revealed expanses of
skin and floated over her lush curves. Danni had always
been something of a tomboy and preferred practicality
along with comfort but she still had feelings and she
had pride and Adam had just dented both. Adam, whose
opinion shouldn't matter to her. But apparently did.

Shock spread over his face. Shock and remorse. He
reached for her then dropped his hand. "Danni, I didn't
mean it like that. I meant I still see you as a kid. It still
surprises me that you're even old enough to have your
license."

She shoved the hurt down, tried to replace it with defiance. "I got my license over a decade ago. And you're not that much older than me."

"I know I'm not. It just feels like it sometimes."

"True." It had always felt that way. Adam had always seemed older. Distant. Unreachable.

He sighed and closed his eyes. When he opened them again he said, "I'm sure you're a fine woman, but it hardly qualifies you to give me dating advice. I've known enough women."

"I'm sure you have," she said quietly. Of late there had been quite the string of them. All of them beautiful, intelligent and worldly, with much to recommend them for the position of future princess. But despite those apparent recommendations, he'd seldom dated the same woman twice. And never, to her knowledge, a third time. She didn't mean to keep track, but a glance at the papers on any given day, even if only when lighting the fire in her father's gatehouse, kept track for her. But it certainly wasn't her place to comment and the implied criticism would centuries ago have cost her her head.

She was thankful for the fact that beheadings hadn't been legal for several centuries because judging by the displeasure in Adam's eyes, he just might have been in favor of the practice right about now. For a moment she actually thought he might lose his legendary cool. She couldn't even feel triumph. There had been a time when, egged on by Adam's younger brother Rafe, flapping the unflappable Adam had been a pastime for the small group of children raised on the palace estate. But she was still too preoccupied with covering her own hurt to feel anything akin to satisfaction.

Adam drew himself taller. The barrier of remoteness shuttered his face, hardened his jaw. "I apologize, Danielle. Unreservedly. Thank you for your services tonight. They won't be required in future."

Sacked. He'd sacked her again.

Danni was still stung by her run-in with Adam the next night as she and her father ate their minestrone in front of the fire. Soup and a movie was their Sunday night tradition.

They finished the first half of the tradition and settled in for the movie. A big bowl of buttery popcorn sat on the coffee table and an action adventure comedy was ready to go in the DVD player, just waiting for her press of the button.

Usually, when she was in San Philippe she came round from her apartment for the evening. But her place was being redecorated so she'd been staying with her father for the last week. She had yet to tell him about the fiasco last night. Tonight would be the perfect opportunity.

But she hadn't fully recovered from the experience.

Although she pretended to herself that she was indifferent, at odd moments the latter part of the evening resurfaced and replayed itself in her head. She should have done everything so differently. Starting with keeping her mouth shut in the first place.

As head driver, her father had a right to know what had happened. Would expect to know. But she hadn't been able to tell him. Because more than head driver, he was her father and he'd be so disappointed in her. And she hated disappointing the man who'd done so much for her and who asked so little of her.

It had occurred to her that if she just kept quiet, he

need never know. It's not as if she'd ever be driving for Adam again.

Besides, her silence was justified because her father was still so saddened by the visit to his friend. She wanted to alleviate, not add, to that sorrow. At least that was her excuse. The movie they were about to watch would be the perfect tonic. The fact that it featured an awesome and realistic car chase scene would be an added bonus. And they'd both once met the main stunt driver.

It didn't matter, she told herself, if she never drove for Adam again. It was such a rare occurrence in the first place it was hardly going to make any difference. And she knew Adam wouldn't let it have any bearing on her father's position within the palace staff. No. Their exchange had been personal. He'd keep it so. That was part of his code.

She'd just found the television remote when three sharp knocks sounded at the door. Her father looked at her, his curiosity matching hers. He moved to stand but Danni held up her hand. "Stay there. I'll get it."

Visitors were rare, particularly without notice. Because her father lived on the palace grounds, in what had once been the gatehouse, friends couldn't just drop by on a whim.

Danni opened the door.

This was no friend.

Two

"Adam." Danni couldn't quite keep the shock from her voice. Was this about last night or was there some further trouble she had gotten into?

"Danielle." His face was unreadable. "I'd like to talk to you. May I come in?"

After the briefest hesitation she stepped back, giving him access. Much as instinct and pride screamed to do otherwise, you didn't refuse the heir to the throne when he asked to come in. But to her knowledge, the last time Adam had been on this doorstep looking for her was fifteen years ago when he and Rafe had turned up to invite her to join in the game of baseball they were organizing. She couldn't quite remember the reason for the game—something to do with a leadership project Rafe had been doing for school. What she remembered with absolute clarity was how badly that endeavor had ended.

Adam stepped into the small entranceway, dominating the space. He smelled good. Reminding her of last night. By rights she should loathe the scent linked with her mortification rather than want to savor it. She heard her father standing up from the couch in the living room behind her.

"St. Claire." Adam smiled at her father. "Nothing important. I wanted a word with Danielle if I may."

"Of course. I'll just pop out to the workshop."

Danni didn't want her father to hear whatever it was Adam was about to say because despite his apparent efforts at geniality it couldn't possibly be good. Nor did she want her father to go because while he was here Adam might actually have to refrain from saying whatever it was that had brought him here.

"Working on another project?" Adam asked.

A smile lit her father's face as he came to join them in the foyer. "A model airplane. Tiger Moth. I should have it finished in a few more months. A nice manageable project." Both men smiled.

Not long after Danni and her father's return to San Philippe when she was five, he'd inherited the almost unrecognizable remnants of a Type 49 Bugatti.

For years the Bugatti had been an ongoing project occupying all of his spare time. It had been therapy for him following the end of his marriage to Danni's mother.

There had been nothing awful about her parents' marriage, aside from the fact that their love for each other wasn't enough to overcome their love for their respective home countries. Her father was miserable in America and her mother was miserable in San Philippe.

And for a few years, after his mother's death, Adam

had helped her father on the car. Danni too had joined them, her primary role being to sit on the workbench and watch and pass tools. And to remind them when it was time to stop and eat. Building the car had been therapy, and a distraction for all of them. She had an early memory of sitting in the car with Adam after her father had finished for the evening. Adam, probably no more than eleven, had entertained her by pretending to drive her, complete with sound effects, to imaginary destinations.

By the time Danni was fifteen none of them needed the therapy so much anymore. Adam, busy with schooling and life, had long since stopped calling around. Her father sold the still unfinished car to a collector. Parts had been a nightmare to either source or make and time had been scarce. Though Danni had later come to suspect, guiltily, that the timing of the sale may have had something to do with the fact that her mother had been lobbying for her to go to college in the States. And fees weren't cheap.

Her father shut the door behind him and she and Adam turned to face one another. Adam's gaze swept over her, a frown creasing his brow. She looked down at her jeans and sweater, her normal casual wear. Definitely not palace standard but she wasn't at the palace.

Silence loomed.

"Sit down." Danni gestured through to the living room and the couch recently vacated by her father.

"No, that's…okay." The uncertainty was uncharacteristic. Seeming to change his mind, Adam walked through to the living room and sat.

Danni followed and sat on the armchair, watching, wary.

"I have to apologize."

Not this again. "You did that."

Adam suddenly stood and crossed to the fireplace. "Not for…that. Though I am still sorry. And I do still maintain that I didn't mean it the way you took it. You're obviously—"

"Then what for?" She cut him off before he could damn her femininity with faint praise.

"For sacking you."

She almost laughed. "It's not my real job, Adam. I have the Grand Prix work. I was covering for Dad as a favor. The loss is no hardship."

"But I need to apologize because I want you to drive for me again."

This time the silence was all hers as she stared at him.

Finally she found her voice. "Thanks, but no thanks. Like I said, the loss was no hardship. I think I demonstrated why I'm the last person you want as your driver."

"Yes, you are the last person I want as my driver because you're so perceptive and so blunt you make me uncomfortable. But unfortunately I think I need you."

She made *him* uncomfortable? And he *needed* her? Curious as she was she wasn't going to ask. His statements, designed to draw her in, to lower her defenses, had all the makings of a trap. Warning bells clamored. She just wanted Adam to leave. "I don't know what you're playing at." She stood up and crossed to him, looking into his face, trying to read the thoughts he kept hidden behind indecipherable eyes. "You don't need me. There are any number of palace drivers, and I don't need the job. Seems pretty clear-cut to me."

"I could ask Wrightson," he said with obvious reluctance.

The younger man her father saw as his chief rival. "Or Dad," she suggested.

He shook his head. "I try not to use your father for the nighttime work."

She knew he did that in deference to her father's age and seniority. But her father wouldn't necessarily see it as a favor. He didn't like to think he was getting older.

"Besides, it's not just driving that I need." Adam studied her for several seconds longer and she could see him fighting some kind of internal battle. Finally he spoke again. "I called Clara this morning to ask her out again."

"You don't think that was too soon?"

"Maybe that's what it was. But I don't have time, or the inclination, for games."

"Oh." Danni's stomach sank in sympathy. This wasn't going to be good. She just knew it.

Adam rested his elbow on the mantel and stared into the fire. "She said she valued my friendship."

"Ouch."

"But that there had been no romance." A frown creased his brow. "No spark."

"Ahh." Danni didn't dare say anything more.

"That I hadn't even looked into her eyes when I was speaking to her. Not properly. That I was too uptight." He looked into Danni's eyes now, as though probing for answers.

"Mmm." She tried desperately to shield her thoughts—that he just had to look at someone with a portion of the intensity he was directing at her, and if that intensity was transformed into something like, oh say, desire, the woman at the receiving end would have only two choices, melt into a puddle or jump his bones. Danni glanced away.

"So—" he took a deep breath and blew it out "—you were right. Everything you said."

"Anyone could have seen it," she said gently.

"Sadly, you're probably right about that, too. The thing is, not anyone would have pointed it out to me. I don't know who else I can trust to be that honest with me and I can't think who else I'd trust enough to let as close as I'm going to have to let you. I can admit my weaknesses to you and you alone because you already seem to know them."

She knew being who he was had to be lonely and undoubtedly more so since Rafe, his closest confidante, had married. The fact that Rafe had married the woman intended as Adam's bride might not have helped either. But he brought much of his isolation on himself. He didn't let people close. And she shouldn't let his problems be hers. But somewhere in there, in the fact that he had a level of trust for her, was a compliment. Or maybe not. Maybe she was the next best thing to another brother.

She didn't know what to say. Her head warned her to just say no.

He was staring at the fire again. "It's imperative that I marry a woman who'll make a good princess, someone who can lead the country with me. And I know what I'm looking for in that regard. I know my requirements."

"Your requirements?" Wasn't that just like him. "Please don't tell me you have a prioritized list somewhere on your laptop."

He looked sharply at her, but spoke slowly. "All right, I won't tell you that."

Danni slapped her head. "You do, don't you?"

"I said I wouldn't tell you."

"For pity's sake, Adam."

A wry smile touched his lips.

"You do need help."

"Not with my list or what's on it. That's nonnegotiable. I just need help with being a better me and a much better date."

She shook her head. "You don't need help being a better you. You just have to let people see the real you, not the *you* that you think you have to be."

He hesitated. "So you'll help me?"

Had she just put her foot into a trap that was starting to close? "I haven't said that. I'd like to, Adam, really I would. But I don't have time. I'm only staying with Dad for a couple more weeks while I'm on leave and my apartment's being redecorated."

He raised his eyebrows. "It's that big a job? Making me into a better date? It's going to require more than a couple weeks?"

"No. I'm sure it's not."

"Then it won't take up much of your time, will it?"

She chewed her lip as she shook her head. When she was ten, Adam, who'd had a broken leg at the time, had taught her to play chess. Over the next few years when he came back on summer vacation he always made time to play her at least once or twice. But no matter how much she'd studied and practiced he'd always been able to maneuver her unawares into a corner and into checkmate.

"For so long I haven't really had to try with women

and...after Michelle I didn't really want to. I've almost forgotten how."

Michelle, whom he'd dated several years ago, well before the advent of Rafe's wife Lexie, was the last woman he'd been linked seriously with. They'd looked like the perfect couple, well matched in so many respects. An engagement had been widely expected. Then suddenly they'd broken up, and Michelle was now engaged to another member of Adam's polo team.

"What about your mystery woman?"

He frowned. Not annoyed, but perplexed. "What mystery woman?"

"Palace gossip has it that..."

"Go on." The frown deepened.

"It doesn't matter."

"Danni? What palace gossip?"

She took a deep breath. "Rumor has it that whenever you get free time, you disappear for an hour or two. When you come back you're generally in a good mood and you've often showered."

The frown cleared from his face and he threw back his head and laughed like she hadn't heard him laugh in years. The sound pleased and warmed her inordinately. "Does this mean there's no mystery woman?" she asked when he stopped laughing.

He was still doing his best to quell his amusement. "There's no woman, mysterious or otherwise."

"Then where—"

"Let's get back on track. Because there does need to be a woman, the right one, and I think you can help. This is important, Danni. All I really want is your insight and a few pointers. It won't take a lot of your time."

Danni hesitated.

"Is there something or…someone you need that time for?"

She didn't want to admit there wasn't. There had been no someone since the rally driver she'd been dating dropped her as soon as he started winning and realized that with success came women—beautiful, glamorous women.

"You'll be compensated."

He correctly interpreted her silence as admission that there wasn't anyone. But the offer of remuneration was insulting. "I wouldn't want that. You wouldn't have to pay me."

"So you'll do it?"

"But you think finding the right woman is about lists and boxes you can check off, and it's not."

"That's why I need you. Lists and tickable boxes are part of it and you'll have to accept that, but I know there's more. I want more." He paused. "I want what Rafe has."

Danni stifled a gasp. "You want Lexie?"

"No." The word was vehement and a look of disbelief and disappointment crossed his face. "I just meant he found someone to marry. Someone he could be happy with."

"She was supposed to be yours," Danni said quietly, daring to voice the suspicion she'd harbored.

"Only according to my father. We, Lexie and I, never had anything." As far as Danni could tell, Adam seemed to be telling the truth and she wanted to believe him. But it was common knowledge that Crown Prince Henri had at one point intended that the American heiress with a distant claim to the throne herself would be the perfect partner, politically, for Adam. "And to be honest," Adam continued, "I'm inclined to believe my father's later assertion that he'd always intended for Lexie and Rafe to be together. He wanted Rafe to settle down and rein in his ways, but he knew Rafe would rebel against any overt matchmaking."

Rafe had been charged with escorting Lexie to San Philippe to meet Adam. By all accounts the two had fought falling in love almost from the time they laid eyes on one another. When Rafe and Lexie finally gave in to their feelings, they utterly derailed the Crown Prince's perceived plans and Rafe's carefree bachelor existence. They'd since married and now had a beautiful baby girl. Rafe had never looked happier. And while to all outward appearances Adam had also seemed more than happy with the arrangement, Danni had always wondered. A little.

He shook his head as he watched her. "You don't believe it?"

She shrugged.

"I like Lexie." He sighed heavily as though this wasn't the first time he'd had to explain himself. "In fact, I love her. But as a sister. It was obvious from the start that it was never going to work for us. We just didn't connect."

"She's beautiful. And vivacious."

"She's both those things. But she wasn't for me. And I wasn't for her."

Danni nodded, almost, but not quite, buying it.

He must have read that shred of doubt in her eyes. "I'll tell you something on pain of death and only because it will help you believe me."

"You don't have to."

"I think I do." Adam glanced away looking almost embarrassed. "On our first date…"

A log shifted and settled in the fire as she waited for him to continue.

"I fell asleep."

She covered her mouth. "No."

"I'd been working hard, putting in some long hours. The timing was off. Dad never should have had her brought out then." He reeled off his excuses. "But anyway, we went to dinner at the same place I went with Clara, we had a lovely meal and on the drive home…" He shrugged. "It was inexcusable. But it happened."

"Was my father driving?"

Adam nodded.

"That explains why he's always been adamant that you were okay with Rafe and Lexie."

"I'm more than okay with it. But I've seen how happy they are, and Rebecca and Logan, as well."

Hard on the heels of his brother finding love his sister, Rebecca, had, as well. Her wedding to Logan, a self-made millionaire from Chicago, would be in two months. "And I wonder…"

"If you can have it, too?" Probably every single person in country had wondered the same thing, the fairy tale come true. Danni certainly had.

He sighed. "It's not realistic though. Not with the life I lead. The constraints on it, constraints that whoever marries me will have to put up with."

He'd deny himself love? Deny himself even the chance at it? And for someone as smart as he was, his reasoning was screwy. "Don't you see? That's why it's more important than ever that there's love. That she knows, whatever the constraints, that you, the real you—" She touched her fingertips just above his heart and the room seemed to shrink. She snatched her hand away. "—are worth it."

Adam's gaze followed her hand. "So, you'll help me?"

Danni hesitated.

A fatal mistake.

"I have a date on Friday." He spoke into the silence of her hesitation. "If you could drive for me then you'll be doing me and my father and the country a favor."

"So it's my patriotic duty?"

"I wouldn't quite put it like that but…" He shrugged. "I don't know if you've heard, but the doctors have told Dad to ease up on work and watch his stress levels. This is one way I can help. So, I need to expedite this process. I want a date for Rebecca and Logan's wedding, and I can't take just anyone. It has to be someone I'm seeing seriously. So that means I need to be working on it now. We've only got two months."

Danni sighed heavily. "See? Your whole approach is wrong. It's not a *transaction* that you can *expedite*. You can't put time limits on things like this."

"This is why I need your help. As a friend."

"You might think you want my help, but I remember you well enough to know that you don't take advice or criticism well. Especially not from me."

"No," he agreed. "But I'm not looking for criticism as such, just pointers."

"You might see my pointers as criticism."

"I'll try not to." Sincere, with the merest hint of a smile.

There was a time when she practically hero-worshipped Adam and would have done anything he asked of her. So she had to fight the unquestioning instinct to agree to his request. Just because it wasn't a big job and she had a little time on her hands didn't mean it was a good idea. She hadn't been this hesitant about anything since her skydiving course last year. She needed to know what she'd be getting into and she needed Adam to know she wasn't that blindly devoted girl anymore. "Normal rules would have to not apply. Because if I agree to do this, there could well be things I want to say to you that usually I absolutely wouldn't."

"This is sounding ominous."

"It won't work if I don't have the freedom to speak my mind."

He hesitated. "If you do this for me, then I'll accept that much." His dark eyes were earnest. "I'd appreciate it, Danni." When she was younger he'd called her Danni. But somewhere along the way as they'd both gotten older, and he'd gone away to school and become even more serious, formality had crept into their relationship and he'd switched to calling her Danielle with rare exceptions. Calling her Danni now brought back recollections of those easier times. He touched a finger to the small bump on his nose. Just briefly. The gesture looked almost unconscious, and she'd seen him make it before. But it never failed to make her feel guilty. Did he know that? Was it part of persuading her that she owed him?

Whether he knew it or not, it worked. "I don't know how much help I can be."

He recognized her capitulation. She could see the guarded triumph in his eyes, the almost imperceptible easing to his shoulders.

"I can't guarantee anything. Like you pointed out, I'm no expert on romance."

"But as *you* pointed out, you are a woman. And I trust you."

She sucked in a deep breath, about to make a last-minute attempt at getting out of this.

"I'll be seeing Anna DuPont. She fits all my criteria. I've met her a couple times socially and I think there's potential for us. Drive for us. Please."

He could, if he chose, all but order her to do it, make it uncomfortable for her or her father if she refused, but his request felt so sincere and so personal—just between the two of them—that the hero worship she'd once felt kicked in and she was nodding almost before she realized it. "One date," she said, trying to claim back some control. "I'll drive you for one date."

Three

On Friday, Danni pulled up to Adam's wing of the palace in the Bentley. The sandstone building towered above her, the shadows seeming to hide secrets and to mock her for how little she knew. What had she gotten herself into? There was no protocol for this situation, for being part driver, part honest adviser, part friend. She took a fortifying breath. All she could do was to stick with what she knew and maybe trust her instincts. At least she wouldn't be expected to guard her tongue quite as closely as normal.

She got out and waited by the passenger door while he was notified of her arrival. On those occasions she had driven for him in the past, he'd been scrupulously punctual. Tonight was no different. As the clock on the distant tower chimed seven, he appeared, stepping out into a pool of light.

Danni looked at him and couldn't figure out whether this was going to be ridiculously easy or ridiculously difficult.

She was still shaking her head as he stopped in front of her. "You have something to say? Already?"

"Yes. You're wearing a suit and tie."

"Yes."

"You're going to have dinner at the riverside jazz festival?"

"Yes." He managed to make that single word of agreement intimidating.

But it was clearly time for some of the honesty he'd said he trusted her to voice. "Nobody wears a suit and tie to a jazz festival."

"I do."

"Not tonight. This is not a state dinner." She held out her upturned palm. "Hand over the tie." For a moment Danni thought he might refuse. "You want my help?"

Gritting his teeth, he loosened his tie and slid it from around his neck. He dropped the strip of fabric into her hand. "Satisfied?"

She closed her fingers around the warm silk. "No."

"No?"

"The top button." She nodded at the neck of his shirt.

His lips pressed together but he reached up, undid the button then dropped his hand and looked at her patiently. Obviously waiting for her approval. But he still didn't look quite right. He still looked tense and formal. A little fierce almost.

"And the next one."

He opened his mouth, about to protest, she was certain, then closed it again and slowly undid the second button.

"Much better," she said. "Just that extra button makes you look far more relaxed, almost casual. In a good way," she added before he could object. She wanted to tousle his hair, mess it up just a little but knew that tousled hair would be a step too far for Adam. Tonight anyway. Maybe they could work on that. She settled for reaching up and spreading his collar a little wider. "See, this vee of chest?" She pointed at what she meant, at what riveted her gaze. "Women like that. It's very appealing."

"It is?"

"Definitely. And you smell really good. That's always a bonus." She was close enough to know. Without thinking she closed her eyes and inhaled. And the image of a shirtless Adam—branded in her memory—came back. The image had lurked there since the incident that had gotten her banned from driving. Her shortcut, the potholes, the spilling of his coffee that had required him to change his shirt in the back of the limo. Oh, yes. She'd seen him shirtless then. An unthinking glimpse in the rearview mirror of a broad contoured torso and sculpted abs. More than appealing. A fleeting moment of stunned and heated eye contact. It was a sight that had left her breathless and slightly dazed and slipped into her dreams. His banning her after that episode had almost been a relief.

She opened her eyes now to find him studying her, curiosity in his gaze and something like confusion. Despite the cool night Danni felt suddenly warmer. This new role was an adjustment for both of them. The normal boundaries of protocol and etiquette had blurred—they had to—but it left her floundering. Maybe she ought not to have admitted with such enthusiasm that his chest was appealing or that he smelled good. But surely if she was going to criticize and point out where she thought he went wrong, then she also needed to point out where she thought he went right.

She reached for his door, opened it wide.

She slipped his tie into her pocket, stepped back and gestured to the open door. "Let's go find your princess."

An hour later boredom was setting in. Just another reason, she reminded herself, why she'd never have made a good chauffeur. No matter how much her father would have liked it for her.

Danni fiddled with the radio again, adjusted her seat and her mirrors, and then leaned over and opened the glove compartment. A white card stood propped up inside. Definitely not regulation. Frowning, she pulled out the card. Across the front in strong sloping letters it read, "Just in case." Behind the card sat a white cardboard box. Curious, Danni pulled it out and opened it. Neatly arranged inside was a selection of gourmet snacks.

The thoughtfulness of the gesture had her grinning and taking back any uncharitable thoughts she'd ever had about Adam.

Another hour passed, during which Danni snacked and read, before Adam and his date walked out of the restaurant. Was that a hint of a stagger to the fashion-model-slender Anna's gait as she laughed and leaned against Adam? Perhaps having so little body fat meant she was just cold and needed to absorb some of his heat.

But the impression Danni got was that there had been no shortage of the champagne that they'd started—at her suggestion—on the way to the restaurant.

Anna somehow managed to stay plastered to Adam as they got into the backseat. At a nod from him—and a brief moment of eye contact, Danni drove off.

At the first set of traffic lights, she glanced in the mirror. And then just as quickly looked away.

Anna apparently had no need for eye contact or poetry. Maybe there had been enough of that in the riverside restaurant. She had undone more of Adam's buttons and had slid her hand into the opening. It certainly didn't appear that anyone was cold anymore. The screen between them blocked out most sound but Danni could hear Anna's laughter, throaty and, Danni supposed, sexy. Some men might like it. Some men apparently being Adam.

She thought of the tie still in her pocket and knew that there was something wrong with her because she wanted to pass it back to him and tell him to put it on. But really, carrying on like that, it was undignified. Then again, it was the sort of thing she'd once expected from Rafe, and never thought it was undignified in his case. But the two brothers were different. They always had been. Adam was all about barriers. And the way the woman in the back had bypassed them didn't seem right.

Danni's only consolation was that it looked like her work here was done. He'd been deluding himself if he'd thought he needed her help and she'd been deluding herself if she'd thought she had any to offer. He didn't need help at all. Anna was doing all the work. And they were both clearly enjoying themselves while she did it. Danni would be able to go home and forget all about Adam Marconi and his search for the right woman.

Her grip on the wheel tight and her jaw even tighter,

Danni pulled to a stop in front of Anna's apartment building. And maybe, just maybe, her stop wasn't quite as gentle as it ought to have been.

The couple in the backseat drew apart. Anna trailed her long red fingernails down the front of Adam's shirt. The green-and-gold-uniformed doorman stepped forward to open the car door and the couple got out, Anna still managing to drape herself over Adam. Danni wasn't sure if she was whispering into Adam's ear or trying to eat it. It looked like the latter. Danni rubbed at her own ear in sympathy.

Not wanting to watch her passengers walk to the doorway of Anna's building—public displays of affection held no appeal—she retrieved her book and reclined her seat. She hadn't even found her page when Adam reappeared and slid into the backseat.

"The palace," he said, the words terse. He lowered the privacy screen but said nothing more as she drove through the city and out toward the palace estates. She chanced the occasional glance at him in the mirror. He hadn't fallen asleep though there was a definite weariness about his eyes as he watched the city slide by.

She knew something of his schedule and so she knew that the days and evenings of the previous week had been hectic and full, meetings after functions after openings and launches.

She eased to a careful stop in front of his wing of the palace and met his gaze in the mirror.

"Better," he said.

"Better? Your date?"

"No. The date was decidedly worse. I meant your stopping. Compared to the one in front of Anna's apartment."

Ahh. "I apologize for that. My foot slipped."

"Thank you."

For apologizing or for her foot slipping in the first place? She wasn't going to ask. By the time she'd walked around the back of the car, he'd opened his door and stood. His gaze slid over her from head to toe.

Usually she was good at the whole calm, stoic thing but Danni fought the urge to squirm under his scrutiny, having no idea what he thought when he looked at her. Or maybe it was just the cold making her want to fidget. It was freezing out here tonight. Cold enough for snow.

Her gaze flicked to Adam's shirtfront, still largely unbuttoned. Frowning, as though only just remembering that they were undone, he reached for the lower buttons and slowly did them up. The movement of his fingers held her mesmerized.

It wasn't till he was finished that she remembered what she needed to say. "Thank you, too," she said. "For the food."

"It was no trouble."

And it wouldn't have been. Someone else would have prepared the food and another person would have put it in the car. But it was Adam who'd had the idea and she was still oddly touched by it.

He slid his hands into his pockets and tilted his head toward the palace. "Come in."

"To the palace?"

"Where else? I don't want to talk about the date out here."

Danni looked around. Assorted staff members stood discreet distances away, always at the ready. If she insisted on staying out here she'd only make everyone colder. Besides, she'd been into the palace before. Many times in fact, though not in the last few years. This should be no different. So she shrugged and walked with Adam, went through the door held open by a staff member she didn't recognize. As Adam led her up a flight of stairs and along a corridor hung with gilt-framed portraits, she realized where they were going.

He opened the door to the library. The room, with its floor-to-ceiling shelves of leather-bound books, and armchairs big enough to curl up in, had been her favorite when she was younger. The chess set they used to play on was still here too, nestled in a corner by a window.

Despite the fact that the room had been designed to be restful, Danni was far from relaxed. It had been years since she was last here and in that time her ease in Adam's company and her confidence in their simple friendship had vanished.

In the car she was in charge, of the car at least. Her father's gatehouse was her territory, too, and outside was…outside. A place of freedom. But here, inside the palace, where everything was governed by rules not of her making and many of them outside of her awareness, standing with the heir apparent, she was out of her depth and well out of her comfort zone.

She walked to a side table and set her cap on it then slowly peeled off her gloves, feeling oddly vulnerable without the protection her uniform afforded her. A protection that said *this is who I am and this is who you are.* We're people defined by our roles. But now, as she raked a hand through her hair, she was just Danni and he was Adam. There could never be a *just* in front of his name unless it was used in its opposite meaning.

He was *just* gorgeous. Serious, but gorgeous with those dark eyes that seemed always to be watching and thinking.

Even without the props of her uniform, she knew she had to keep focused on her reason for being here—which had nothing to do with Adam's eyes. Although maybe the eyes had helped sway her, subliminally at least. "So, your date?"

"Let's wait till after dessert."

"Dessert?"

She turned at the sound of a tap on the door. A footman walked in carrying a tray, set it on the low table between two armchairs and then left.

Danni glanced from the tray to Adam.

"I thought you might be hungry."

"Not that hungry!" She looked at the twin slices of cheesecake and the two mugs of cream-topped hot chocolate.

He smiled his first smile of the evening. "It's not all for you."

"But you've just eaten."

He shook his head. "Anna was a salad-only type of woman. No carbohydrates. No dressing. I was hardly going to eat dessert while she'd scarcely touched a thing. As it was, her pushing her lettuce around her plate all evening almost put me off my linguine. And I love linguine. So aside from it being bad manners, I was in no hurry to prolong the evening. By the time the waiter asked if we wanted to order dessert, the future chances for a relationship were crystal clear."

"You've already fed me once tonight." Her mouth watered even as she pretended that she wasn't hungry.

"It was a long evening and that was just a snack. And

unless things have changed drastically from when you were younger, you have—let's call it a healthy appetite and a sweet tooth. And cheesecake was a particular favorite." He watched her. "Have things changed?"

A grin tugged at her lips and her gaze strayed back to the cheesecake. "Apparently not all that much."

He picked up the two bowls. "Sit down then."

Once she was settled in an armchair he passed her a bowl and took the opposite chair.

Danni bit into the tart velvety cheesecake and her eyes almost rolled back in her head in ecstasy while she savored the delight. "Charlebury's still chef?" she asked once she'd opened her eyes again.

Adam laughed. "Yes."

For the next few minutes they ate in appreciative silence. Finally, sated and the dessert finished, Danni set down her bowl.

"Not licking it?" Adam asked, teasing in his tone.

"Trust me, I thought about it. I have only one complaint."

He asked the question with his eyes.

"I don't think I'm going to be able to do the hot chocolate justice now."

"You'll give it your best shot, though?"

"It would be cowardly of me not to at least try. But I think I have to stand and give it a few minutes before I make the attempt." She crossed to one of the long vertical windows. A single snowflake drifted past the narrow pane of glass, lonely and aimless.

The grounds close to the palace were well lit but farther out, the light faded to shadows illuminated only sporadically by pools of brightness for either security or decoration or both. Occasional statues and trees stood spotlighted. And in the distance a building… "I think I can see the gatehouse."

"Beyond the stand of trees to the west?"

"Yes. I don't remember being able to see it from the library."

He lifted a shoulder. "It's been a while since you were here. You're taller."

"I guess. The lights are still on," she said turning her gaze back to the window. "That probably means Dad's fallen asleep watching TV again."

"Do you remember the first time I saw you in here?"

"I try not to." Ever since he mentioned the word *taller* she'd wanted to steer the conversation in a different direction. She watched his reflection in the glass. He frowned. "I'm still a little embarrassed. I remember what I said."

His frown eased to a smile. "That just because I was taller and could reach the higher books and just because I was a prince, didn't make me any better than you."

"Yeah, that. Thanks for the reminder."

He was still smiling, with his eyes at least. "You're welcome."

"I had a little chip on my shoulder."

"No kidding."

"I was new here. Feeling out of place, and a little, no, a lot, intimidated and insecure."

"I knew that."

Danni turned back to him. "You were good to me, telling me that you were glad I didn't think of you as any different because you were a prince, because so many people did treat you differently." Danni laughed. "And then you said that maybe being taller made you a little bit better though." She pointed to a shelf. "Look.

The atlas is still up there. You helped me find America on it. Asked about where I'd come from." He had the people skills even then that made him such a good prince today, made him so well loved by his countrymen.

"I don't want to tarnish my image, but I was supposed to be studying and didn't want to. You were my excuse not to."

She remembered him sitting at the desk, books spread all over it. To her, at five years old, his ten years had made him look almost grown up. Ultimately, the fact that he became her protector and champion till she found her feet had indebted her to him.

For a long time after that she'd worshipped him, refusing to hear a hint of a bad word spoken, even in jest, about him by any of the other palace children.

"So, your date?" Danni prompted, looking back at him. That was why she was here. To help him find the right woman. Not to reminisce. She could return that favor he'd done her all those years ago.

Tension crept back into his shoulders. She ought not to be thinking about smoothing her hand over his brow, or massaging those broad shoulders. "You said the date was worse? I have to say, from where I sat, it looked to be going remarkably well."

Adam shook his head. "Appearances can be deceiving. It turned out we weren't all that compatible. I realized I'd left an important criterion off my list."

"Being?"

"A certain restraint in the consumption of alcohol."

Adam picked up the hot chocolates and carried them over to her. Danni reached for one, wrapping her fingers around the mug. "Anna could just have been nervous. She might actually be shy and reserved and conservative. Maybe she was so nervous she drank more than she would have normally. You can be intimidating."

"Not on a date. At least I try not to be," he added, forestalling her argument.

"There wasn't a lot to her, it wouldn't take much alcohol. And if she was shy…"

"That occurred to me," Adam said, standing shoulder to shoulder with her and looking out into the night. "But the suggestions she made as to how we might carry on with our date didn't seem entirely consistent with someone shy and reserved, or the least bit conservative."

Danni didn't want to imagine. "You didn't take her up on them? Because from what I saw you didn't seem entirely unhappy with the situation."

Adam turned his head and his grin had an endearing boyishness to it. "I had a beautiful woman in my lap wanting to take advantage of me. Of course I wasn't unhappy. And I didn't want to be rude."

"Of course not. Always the gentleman. But?"

The smile dimmed, turned serious. "There was no real chemistry. Not when we talked. Not even when we kissed. So, aside from the fact that she was well on her way to being drunk, there was never going to be a second date. Although she claimed that didn't bother her, it wouldn't have been…right."

Danni didn't analyze her relief or why his sense of honor pleased her quite so much. "She might not have been such a good look in a future crown princess, either."

"No."

"And your father wouldn't have approved."

"Ahh, no."

"So it worked out for the best."

"Yes."

"And clearly you don't actually need my services. Anna certainly found you attractive at least."

"Anna was drunk."

"I don't think that's necessary for a woman to find you attractive." In fact she knew it wasn't. Not a drop of alcohol had passed Danni's lips and she had no trouble finding him attractive. Too much so. His eyes, his lips, his chest—so much about him fascinated her. Which was why it might be best if they ended this arrangement.

"I know it's not. But being serious about the process certainly takes the fun out of it."

"Well of course it does if you approach it with the determination and precision of a military exercise. What was the last fun date you went on?"

"I'm not discussing past dates with you, Danni."

"You wanted my help."

"With future dates not past ones."

"But maybe if you told me about the ones that worked. Or about Michelle."

"No."

And maybe she didn't really want to know about past successful dates. She just needed to help him find a solution to his current dilemma. "So find a woman who enjoys the same things as you and do some of them together. That way you know you'll both at least have fun even if it doesn't turn into anything more."

Adam nodded as though considering her suggestion but said nothing.

"So what do you enjoy doing?" she prompted.

"I hardly remember," he said with a frown and a shake of his head that implied he didn't think it was all that important. "It's been so long since I did anything just for the fun of it. That's not what my life is about now."

"And it shows."

"Care to explain?"

Did she imagine that hint of tightness in his voice? "You don't need me to explain. And it wasn't a criticism."

"Much."

"It was a statement. You carry the weight of the world on your shoulders, you do everything you can for your family and the country, and you don't seem to do anything just for you. Just for the pure enjoyment of it. A little impulsiveness every now and then wouldn't kill you. All work and no play..."

"I play polo," he said triumphantly. "When my schedule allows," he added.

"I've seen you and the way you play—" she shook her head "—that's not anyone's definition of fun. You play as intensely as you work."

"But I enjoy it."

"It still doesn't make for much of a date for anyone else. And it's too structured. What about doing things on impulse? For laughs, for fun. Read my lips. Fun. F.U.N. Fun."

His gaze seemed to fix on her mouth as she spoke, and his frown returned. Why did he so often frown when he looked at her? She got the feeling he wasn't even listening to her.

There had been something else she was going to

add, but words and thought evaporated, replaced by an awareness she couldn't repress. Awareness of standing here with Adam. Close enough to touch. Awareness of the fact that although he'd fastened some of his buttons, he still had too many undone for her comfort, some of which he'd undone at her insistence. Awareness of that glimpse of chest, which was even more appealing than it had been earlier in the evening. And of the way he smelled—divine.

Four

Adam looked at Danni and felt himself leaning closer. He knew all about impulse—and about fighting it. Impulse told him to kiss her, to pull her into his arms and silence her with his lips on hers.

That would be pure enjoyment.

Far more even than watching her devour the cheesecake. He'd wanted some way of showing he appreciated what she was doing for him; feeding her had seemed like the perfect solution. But she ate with such uncensored sensual pleasure that he'd quickly come to regret the gesture.

The urge to kiss her now shocked him but he wouldn't let it overly concern him. His life was all about *not* acting on impulse. It was about always considering options and consequences before taking action.

But in a perverse way, it was as though since he'd

become serious about finding a wife, his subconscious was trying to thwart him, like a man looking to buy a nice safe Volvo who suddenly sees the perfect tempting Ferrari for sale.

He reminded himself that he'd known Danni since they were kids. It sent a jolt of surprise through him every time he looked at her and realized anew that she was most definitely no longer a kid.

After the evening with Anna, Danni's sparkle, her directness, her innocence were tempting him in ways that she could have no idea about. She wore no lipstick but even without her prompting to read her lips, he was most definitely thinking about them. Soft and mobile. About how the tiny smear of hot chocolate above her top lip would taste, laced with her freshness.

Her green eyes widened as he watched her and he could only hope his thoughts didn't show. Because he couldn't have thoughts like that about her. Because she was Danni.

But if she'd been any other woman, he would have reached for her and kissed that hot chocolate away.

He shook his head to clear it and stepped back, fighting the compulsion to step forward instead. Could her skin possibly feel as soft as it looked? "Danni."

Her gaze was steady on him, a measure of the confusion he felt seemed to shimmer there. She cleared her throat. "Yes."

"You have hot chocolate on your lip."

"Oh." Her quick burst of laughter held uncertainty and she glanced away. Adam passed her a napkin from the tray. "Thank you." She dabbed away the hot chocolate. He almost regretted its loss. But if it stopped him thinking about Danni's lips in ways he had no right to be thinking, then it could only be a good thing.

When he'd woken in the car the first time she drove for him the other night, with her leaning in close, smelling of mint and the cool night, he'd been swamped by an instinctive reaction of purely primal desire. The sort that had been blatantly missing from his date with Clara. It had kicked in before he'd thought to stop it.

And then, before he'd had time to rationalize it, he'd covered his unwanted response with cool civility. He'd tried to create distance and barriers. But he'd been so disconcerted that he spoke without realizing how she might interpret his words. And he'd hurt her. She was one hundred percent the woman he'd claimed he didn't see her as. No matter how desperately he wanted that claim to be true.

She watched him now, waiting for him to speak. "As for fun." That had been what they'd been talking about, hadn't it? "I don't think there's time for that right now."

She took a few steps away, putting a distance he simultaneously regretted and welcomed between them. That distance helped him think a little more clearly, and if he kept his gaze from her petite curves, it helped even more. The uniform she wore did her no favors but he'd seen those curves lovingly revealed by nothing more elegant than jeans and a soft sweater when he'd called at the gatehouse.

"You're kidding. Right?" Her eyes danced with ever-present intelligence and passion and a hint of mockery. Fortunately some things about her hadn't changed—the way she spoke her mind and the way she challenged him. Mostly he appreciated her frankness. Mostly. Other times it drove him nuts.

"This is a serious business."

"I get that," she said with a condescension he hadn't heard anybody use on him in a long time.

"Of course the woman and I need to enjoy each other's company. I want to like her, a lot, and to eventually love her, but I haven't got time to dither and get sidetracked. I'd like to be seeing someone by the time Rebecca and Logan get married. Whoever I take to that wedding will immediately come under public scrutiny. And just because I can have fun with a woman doesn't mean she's going to be suitable as a partner." If only it was that easy.

Danni sighed. "So, *fun to be with* isn't anywhere on your list of criteria."

He heard and ignored the criticism in her tone. "No."

"That explains Clara I guess."

"Clara was very nice."

"You have to admit, even if she didn't want fun, she wanted romance."

"Apparently. And I take the blame for that." He hadn't seen that one coming. "In my defense, Clara had seemed more than happy to discuss weighty issues. She was the one who introduced most of the more serious topics throughout our evening."

"Mmm-hmm." Two syllables laden with cynicism and reproof.

He sighed. Her skepticism was warranted. "The thing is, in political situations I'm good at interpreting mixed messages and subtext. I look for it. I just hadn't realized the extent to which I'd need those skills for dating. I don't *want* to have to use those skills while dating."

"It's just about listening, Adam, about not being totally fixated on your own agenda." She set down her hot chocolate. "If your work is all seriousness, then doesn't that make it more important than ever for you to have someone who can remind you to have fun occasionally, someone who's fun to be with?"

"I can see your point but you're missing mine. Besides, my list of criteria is my decision."

"You're not interviewing job candidates."

Adam said nothing.

"You're not!"

He cleared his throat. "It doesn't seem like an unreasonable way to approach it."

He could see that she wanted to argue but she bit her lip and long seconds later limited herself to a patient, "What else is on your list?"

"Just the usual."

She laughed. The sound, light and almost infectious, broke the tension. How did she make what a moment ago had seemed perfectly reasonable suddenly seem ludicrous? "There is no usual, Adam. People have preferences but they don't *usually* have such rigidly official lists of criteria in the first place."

"How on earth do they expect to find the right person?" His days and weeks were so full that he lived them by lists. They'd served him well so far.

She shrugged. "They just know. Like Rafe and Lexie just knew and Rebecca and Logan just knew. Without lists."

"It seems unreliable. I can't trust in anything as nebulous as *just knowing*."

She shook her head in reluctant defeat. "So spill—what's on your list?"

He hesitated.

"Maybe I know someone suitable."

His list made sense but he knew that Danni would somehow make it seem to not make sense. But it was his list and it didn't matter what Danni St. Claire, pest from his childhood, thought of it, so long as she helped him.

"She'll need to speak multiple languages." How had it come to this? He was sharing his dating woes with Danni. His driver. Next he'd be asking the head gardener how to manage diplomatic appointments.

"I guess I can see why you'd want that," she said.

Despite her words he didn't believe her; there was a light in her eyes he couldn't quite trust.

"You can argue and make love in a range of languages. That'll give variety, that's important. It'll keep things fresh."

He'd known she wasn't taking this seriously. "It's not for the purposes of arguing or making love. I attend endless diplomatic functions with dignitaries from around the world."

Danni was grinning at him.

"You're winding me up, aren't you?"

"You do leave yourself wide open for it. Anyway, like I said, you clearly don't need me driving for you, or giving you advice. You're managing and I don't think we're going to agree on anything important."

"No," he said slowly.

"So, I'll get going." She turned away and headed for the table to get her hat and gloves.

"I wasn't agreeing with you, I was disagreeing."

Slowly, she turned back and a smile quirked her lips. "You usually are."

Which was exactly the kind of comment he expected from her. "Anna was clearly a mistake."

"That might be one area where we agree."

"But she's not the type of woman I expect to be dating in future. I don't think there's going to be anyone else quite as...forward as her on the list. At least I hope not." If Danni didn't stop grinning at him he really was going to have to kiss her. He turned back to the window. "And I'll admit you were right about the tie." The tie she'd made him take off, practically ordering him to undress.

He shook his head sharply, disallowing the sudden image that wanted to insinuate itself there. He rested his fists on the window ledge and stared into the night. "A college education." Focus. He had to stay focused. "Preferably post graduate. Preferably international."

"Go on," he heard her say and could discern nothing of her thoughts from her voice. That was probably a good thing.

"A good conversationalist, a good hostess, diplomatic."

"Of course. Anything else?"

"She'll need to be good with the press and the public, especially children."

"What about looks?"

"Tall, slim, attractive, graceful."

"Hair color?" There was something different about her voice, something controlled. Which wasn't like Danni at all.

"It makes no difference."

"Big of you." That had definitely been a hint of anger in her voice.

He turned to see her standing with her hands on

her hips, her gaze narrowed on him and her lips thin. "What have I done now?" he asked.

She dropped her hands to her sides and shook her head. "You honestly have no idea, do you."

"I have no idea why you're suddenly so angry, like a vengeful pixie, when all I did was answer the questions you asked. You were worried about me not taking criticism well but it seems to be you who's not handling the honesty."

"I'm outraged on behalf of all women."

"Why? Because I have criteria? You can't tell me women don't do that. Must be tall, must be good-looking, must not have a beard, must drive a luxury car and be able to support the lifestyle I'd like to have."

"It's not what was on it that I objected to, it's what you left off. What about kindness, Adam? A sense of humor? What about love and someone you can just be with in the quiet moments of your life? All these criteria you have, they're just more of your barriers."

"I don't have barriers."

She laughed. At him. "You have more barriers than we'll need for the Grand Prix."

"I do not."

"You do. And they're all designed to stop people seeing the real you. You only want them to see the prince, a leader. But, trust me, you don't want to marry someone who sees you like that. You want a companion for life, not a subject. You don't want someone who's going to jump to do your bidding, who says only what you want to hear."

"Actually, that might be pleasant. Surely it would be better than living with someone who constantly challenged and provoked me."

"I give up. There's no point in me doing this, I can't help you if you won't even try."

She headed for the door. But the Danni he remembered from the days they'd played chess and the times they'd played baseball never gave up. Ever. She wasn't bluffing, she was mad. He thought quickly. "Skiing."

She stopped and looked back at him, her eyes narrowed in suspicion.

"I enjoy skiing. It's…fun." Even the word sounded frivolous and insubstantial.

Her smile reappeared and felt like a reward. "See, that wasn't difficult, was it?"

It hadn't been as easy as it should have been. Maybe she was right and he'd become a complete bore. "I'm not a frivolous person."

She crossed back toward him. "Nobody wants you to be. It's part of your appeal. But all work and no play…"

She'd used the word *appeal* or *appealing* in conjunction with him before. And she looked at him now as though there was something there that intrigued her. There was most definitely something in her that intrigued him.

And he had to quash it.

"So, you'll drive me and a date of my choice to the mountains next weekend?" Focus on the task at hand. That was all he had to do.

She shook her head. "I only agreed to drive for you once."

"I'll make it worth your while."

Her gaze narrowed on him as though she was affronted. "I'm not that mercenary."

"You used to be," he said evenly, not buying the mock offense.

Her grin slipped out. "When I was *ten* and only because my Dad never gave me pocket money and you and Rafe always had some. You'd pay for anything that you didn't want to do yourselves." She smiled, perhaps remembering the same things he was, the errands she'd run for them.

"I have more pocket money now." He winked at her.

She seemed as surprised by the gesture as he was. He hadn't winked at anyone in a very long time. But somehow Danni made the years slip away. He touched the bridge of his nose.

She sighed heavily. "I'll drive for you if you promise never to touch your nose again."

"Pardon?"

"You do it deliberately to make me feel guilty. So that I'll do what you want."

"How on earth does my touching my nose make you feel guilty?"

She rolled her eyes. "Because every time you touch that little bump, I remember how you got it in the first place."

"Really? And it makes you feel guilty? But it was an accident. As much my fault as yours." He'd been sixteen and she'd only been eleven. But she'd had a hell of a swing with the baseball bat. And he'd been distracted. He'd been arguing with Rafe instead of paying attention to a game he hadn't even really wanted to be a part of. The ball had come out of nowhere. That was the only time he'd ever seen Danni cry. Not because she'd been hurt but because she'd hurt him. And then she got mad at him for making her cry.

"I know that. But I still feel guilty about it."

"So, if I do this—" he touched the bump "—and

ask nicely, will you drive for me this weekend? Please, Danni."

"Don't. That's not fair."

He touched the bump again. "It's actually hardly noticeable. I don't see it when I look in the mirror, I can scarcely feel it."

"Adam. You're playing dirty."

"No, seriously. Touch it. It's nothing. I think you're imagining it." He reached for her, circling his fingers around her wrist—she had such delicate wrists, like the rest of her—and he lifted her hand.

Curiosity lit her eyes and she bit her bottom lip as she ever-so-tentatively touched the bridge of his nose. Her fingers were so close that he couldn't focus on them but he could see her eyes, could see a certain longing in them. Her lips were softly parted and she smelled as sweet as the promise of spring.

And, damn, there was that urge again. The one that would have him pull her into his arms. He shifted his grip from her wrist and grasped her hand instead and pressed a kiss to the back of it. That was as much as he could allow himself.

And apparently more than she wanted. She pulled her hand free. Hid it behind her back. A fierce blush heated her cheeks.

"You know, maybe it is a little sore still, you could kiss it and make it better." Where had the words come from, the teasing?

"Don't play games with me, Adam." Sudden anger tinged her voice, taking him aback. "I know I'm not sophisticated. But you know it, too. So do not make fun of me. You're better than that."

"Make fun of you? Danni, I'd never. The one time I

tried it, when you were about seven, you kicked me in the shins."

"You just did," she said. The anger had gone, only to be replaced by suspicion.

Usually he communicated well, allowing for no misunderstanding. He'd soothed ruffled diplomatic feathers on many occasions. How was he making such a mess of this when it should be so simple? "No." Making fun of her had been the very last thing on his mind. He'd wanted to kiss her and had settled, at great cost, for her hand instead. Because kissing her, when she was effectively a member of his staff, when he was on the lookout for a wife, and when she was…Danni, would be all kinds of wrong. But he could still feel the cool imprint of her skin on his lips. And that chaste, courtly gesture had stirred far more than the kiss he'd shared with Anna earlier this evening.

"I've offended you and I'm sorry." He needed time to make it better. To get their relationship back to where it ought to be, amiable and respectful.

"You haven't offended me. I'm not that soft."

He liked her indignation, the stubborn tilt to her chin.

"I have offended you, I can see it."

"You haven't. Believe me."

"Prove it. Drive for me next weekend."

She gave a little gasp and her eyes narrowed. "You've done it again, haven't you? You've manipulated me halfway to saying yes and I'm not even sure how you did it."

"I wouldn't try to manipulate you."

"I know. You do it without trying."

Had he? He hadn't meant to. "You're free to drive

for me or not. But I'd really like it if you would." She'd been right about Clara, she'd been right about the tie.

She opened her mouth.

"It'll be the last time, I promise," he said before she could deny him, because suddenly this seemed important. "You see things differently from me. In a good way. So, I'm taking your advice seriously. I'm going to go skiing and I'm going to have fun."

"Whether you like it or not?"

"Exactly." He tried to keep a straight face.

She laughed, breaking the tension he'd caused when he'd kissed her hand. The familiar sparkle returned to her eyes. "This will definitely be the last time. After that, you're on your own and you can take your fun as seriously as you like."

"You'll be able to pick me up next Friday at two?" He had to get her final commitment while he could.

"Okay."

A frown pleated her brow and she imbued that small word with a world of reluctance, but she'd agreed. That was all that mattered.

"Who are you taking?"

"I haven't decided yet. There are a number of prospective candidates."

"Hmmph. Who meet all your criteria?"

"Yes."

"Are their names in a list?"

He said nothing.

"Can I see it?"

He folded his arms.

"Why not leave earlier than two? Let the fun start sooner?"

"I have meetings in the morning."

She didn't roll her eyes, but he thought it might have taken effort on her part not to. She headed for the table and picked up her cap and gloves.

"And don't worry about the uniform. This is definitely outside of regular palace business. We'll be friends."

"That's what worries me. It feels like the ground is shifting and I don't know where I stand."

He held the door for her. "Since when did you ever *not* like a challenge?"

"Since you started using them to work against me."

She reached into her pocket and pulled out the tie he'd forgotten about. He reached for it, and for a second they were connected by that strip of silk. The fabric had been subtly warmed by her body. Her gaze flicked to his and then quickly away as she released the tie. "See you Friday."

"Thank you, Danni. You won't regret it."

She shook her head. "I already do."

Five

"There's a café up ahead." Adam's voice broke through Danni's concentration, snapping her awareness to him.

"Yes," she said warily. They'd been on the road for a little more than an hour and those were almost the first words he had spoken to her since informing her that they'd meet his date there later this evening. And the statement gave her an ominous sinking feeling sapping the pleasure she'd found in the drive. So far, he'd used the time sitting in the back making and taking calls and working on his laptop. It was an arrangement that suited her just fine and she'd hoped he was setting the tone for the whole weekend.

"Let's stop."

A glance in the mirror showed her that his laptop was now shut. Working, he was remote and safe. It was when he leaned back in his seat and focused his attention on her that things, in her head at least, became decidedly unsafe.

"Let's not stop." If she was here as more of a friend than a driver she was allowed to voice an opinion. "It's not planned. I haven't called ahead."

"They'll cope, I'm sure. I don't know what you're going to have but I only wanted a coffee. And maybe a muffin."

"I meant for security. Which you knew. They like to know in advance where we intend stopping." Now, he'd decided to tease? She didn't think much of his timing but the glint in his eyes and the lift to his lips made her stomach give a funny little lurch.

"It'll be okay," he said. "If we didn't know we were stopping, no one else could have. This whole weekend is going to be as low-key and as off-the-radar as possible."

"In that case, we shouldn't stop where people will see you and recognize you." The café loomed ahead. One more minute and they'd pass it.

"Stop the car, Danni."

Repressing a sigh, she pulled off the road and into the parking lot. There was only so far she could push the friend-versus-driver split.

"You wanted me to be more spontaneous."

So now this was her fault? "I don't think I said that, Your Highness." She used the "Your Highness" deliberately. She was desperate to get the formality back into their relationship because something fundamental had shifted that night in the library with him. When he'd kissed her hand, the press of his lips igniting a low forbidden heat. Actually, it had shifted in the seconds before when she'd touched his nose, when her eyes had met his as she did so. She'd been slammed by a desperate desire to kiss him. Properly. To slide into his arms, press herself against him and kiss the bejeebers out of him. Really, she'd been no better than Anna and hadn't even had the excuse of alcohol. If that was spontaneity, it was a bad, bad thing.

"Call me *Your Highness* again and I'll sack you on the spot."

He was joking. About the sacking part anyway. She was sure of it. Just not the "Your Highness" part. He hated that from her. "Fine. I didn't say I wanted you to be more spontaneous. Adam."

The twitch of his lips stretched into a smile. She hadn't realized it before but that smile of his could be irritating, especially when the smugness of someone who'd gotten his way—again—gleamed in his eyes. Even so it made her own lips curve in response.

"No. But you implied it," he said. "So I'm going to be spontaneous. And we're going to stop for unplanned coffee."

"Paul won't like it." Paul was the head of palace security. They'd had a half-hour meeting together before she'd picked up Adam this morning.

Everything was shifting. Even the fact that he'd insisted she not wear her uniform disturbed her. She wasn't used to driving Adam wearing jeans and a sweater. It felt…disconcerting, like she didn't quite know who she was or what role she filled. It blurred the boundaries in her mind. It allowed her to think of Adam and kissing in the same thought. Perhaps she should have packed the uniform just to be safe.

"Paul will cope. Now, are you going to come in with me, or are you going to sit out here in the car and sulk?"

"I don't sulk."

"Good. Let's go get coffee."

Danni got out and muttered a "yes, Your Highness" under her breath. By the time she'd got round to Adam's side of the car he was already standing, breathing deeply of the crisp air. "One day..." she said.

He waited for her to continue, a smile still tilting his lips.

"Yes?"

"One day I'm going to outmaneuver you."

The smile widened and stole her breath. "And on that day Satan will swap his pitchfork for a snow shovel."

She shook her head and turned away, breaking the direct line of fire of that smile. She'd forgotten, or maybe never realized because she'd known him forever, how attractive he really was. Especially when he smiled. But now wasn't when she wanted to be noticing things like that. Now, when she already felt the ground slipping and tilting beneath her. Irritation was the emotion she should be after. Irritation that he thought he could so easily best her. Irritation that it was so often true.

Inside the café they ordered drinks and chocolate muffins and sat at a booth with a view over the pine-forested hillside and up to the snow-covered mountains.

"You can see these mountains from my office in the palace," he said, leaning back in his seat after his first sip of coffee. "Every time I see them I remind myself that I ought to come up here. Rafe and Lexie have been up to the Marconi chalet several times and even Rebecca and Logan have visited. But it's been years since I made the time. So, thank you."

Danni shrugged. "Pleased to be of assistance." More pleased than she could let him know. Already he looked different, a little less strained. This could be her service to the country. Though right now she didn't care about the country, just about him and that this would be good for him. He looked relaxed and open. "So, who's the date?" She needed to remind herself what was really going on here because she was in imminent danger of forgetting. He hadn't told her anything. Just that whoever she was would already be up at the chalet.

"Claudia Ingermason."

"The figure skater?" The Claudia Ingermason Danni was thinking about had won a medal for San Philippe two winter Olympics ago and had since launched her own brand of top-of-the-line winter and ski gear. She was also stunningly beautiful with the looks of a Swedish supermodel.

He nodded. "Rebecca set it up. Claudia's an old school friend of hers. You said to try dating someone I could have fun with. We both enjoy skiing. So it should be...fun."

"You've met her before though?"

"Not exactly."

"So, this is a blind date?"

"No. I know who she is."

"Did you bully Rebecca into setting you up with someone?"

"I resent the implication that I bully people. And even if I tried, Rebecca would be the last person to stand for it. I asked her if she could think of anyone and she came up with Claudia."

"Sounds perfect." Danni set down her coffee. "So why don't we get going? The sooner I get you up there, the sooner you and Claudia can start having fun."

"There's no rush. She's tied up in a photo shoot for her next season's line. It's running behind schedule. She'll be an hour behind us at least." Adam's hands were wrapped around his mug and he didn't appear in any hurry to go. "There's just one thing I don't understand."

"What?"

"Why this still feels like work?"

"Because you're making it work. You're trying to force it."

"I'm just trying to speed things up."

She shook her head. "Relax. If you remember how. If it's meant to be with Claudia, it'll work out. And if it's not, at least you still got to go skiing. But either way I think we should get going because I don't like the look of the weather." The distant clouds seemed to have grown darker in the time they'd been sitting here.

Adam frowned. "You've had a weather update?"

"It's not supposed to snow till much later this evening or possibly tomorrow."

"That's what I thought." He shrugged and took a sip of his coffee. His eyes drifted closed in a long slow blink. And given that this was the most relaxed she'd seen him in years, Danni wasn't going to hurry him along. He'd been out till the early hours of the morning at a state function and from a comment he'd made earlier, it sounded as though he'd scarcely gone to bed because of calls to the other side of the world he'd had to take.

* * *

"What are you doing?" Danni asked, horrified, fifteen minutes later as Adam got into the front seat beside her. She'd been looking forward to the subtle reprieve from his company. Company she could like too much. Now he was beside her instead of in the back, preventing her from putting things into their proper perspective. Me driver, you passenger. Me commoner, you royalty.

Now, as he sat beside her, she had bad thoughts like me woman, you man instead.

"What does it look like?"

"It looks like you've forgotten where you're supposed to sit."

"Where I'm *supposed* to sit? It's *my* car. I can sit anywhere I want."

Definitely man, and one who thought he could do whatever he wanted. Probably because he usually could. Time for diplomacy.

"And a very nice car it is, too. But I'm your driver. And the point of having a driver is so that you can sit in the back and work. Use your time efficiently. Not have to worry about conversation." Like he had done for the first hour of their trip when he was completely oblivious to her. They had each had their space.

"We agreed that this wasn't a normal driving role. You're also here as a friend and adviser. Besides, I've finished what I need to do for the time being. Now, I thought I'd sit up here. The view's better." He looked at her as he spoke so she kept her gaze where it ought to be, trained on the road as it wound up into the mountains. Though if she was able to look at him, she might be better able to gauge what he was playing at. Or not.

She never knew with Adam. By all accounts no one did. She'd often heard his brother and sister, and even once his father—from whom he'd inherited the trait—complain of that very same thing.

He opened the glove compartment.

"What are you doing?"

"I like seeing what you keep in here."

"Nothing."

He pulled out the thriller she was reading, turned it over. "Doesn't look like nothing."

"Nothing you'd be interested in. Adam?"

"Yes?"

"You're sure you haven't got work you should be doing?"

With a smile he closed the glove compartment. "I'm sure. The truth is I'm having second thoughts about this date. Not the skiing part, but the having to get to know another woman."

"It's because you're still looking at this as work."

"It's partly that but worse than that, I've realized that if the chemistry's not right, it's just going to be a waste of my time, like getting stuck in an unproductive meeting."

"Nothing like anticipating success."

"What if it's blatantly obvious there's going to be nothing between us? I should have stuck to dinner. There's an easy escape. So, just so you know—" he folded his arms across his chest "—I'm blaming you if this goes badly."

"If that makes you feel better."

"You know I wouldn't blame you," he said a few moments later.

"I'm not so sure of it. But I can live with it."

She loved the little smile that played at his lips.

They lapsed into silence, and finally Adam seemed content to sit and absorb the beauty and serenity of their surroundings. Snow blanketed the ground and weighed on the branches of the fir trees that stretched back from the road. He spoke only once, to point out the tracks of a deer disappearing into the forest. She could almost feel the tension leeching from him.

His phone rang. The call was brief. He gave assurances to whoever was on the other end of the call that everything was fine and that there was no need to apologize. When the call ended he tipped his head back in the seat. "That solves that. Turn the car around."

Danni flicked a glance at him.

"We're going back."

"Is something wrong?"

"Claudia can't make it. The art director walked out and the photo shoot's in chaos. If she's not going to be there, then there's no point in me going. Besides now I can attend tomorrow's meeting of the Prince's Trust."

"I thought you were pleased to have a good reason not to attend."

"I was, but I don't have that reason anymore."

"But the skiing?"

"The mountain's not going anywhere. I'll come up some other time."

"You haven't in how many years?"

"I will." He wouldn't, and her heart sank on his behalf. Partly because Claudia wasn't going to be there but mainly because he'd miss out on the first day he'd taken off in nearly a year. The lines of tension and weariness showed around his eyes. "You've got competent people at the meeting for you?"

"Yes."

"Then why not stick to your half of the plan and enjoy the skiing? If you take care of your own needs, you're a better leader because of it."

"There are more important things I should be doing."

"But—"

"What?"

"Nothing." It wasn't her place to comment on his private life. He'd ignore her anyway.

"No. What were you going to say?"

"Just that I can't turn around here. There are too many blind corners. There's a place up ahead just a few minutes."

"Good." He tilted back his seat and closed his eyes. Within minutes his face softened and his breathing slowed and deepened, and now, finally asleep, he looked almost to be smiling.

It was an hour later before he opened his eyes again. And for the last half hour Danni's regret over her decision had been growing. Especially the last ten minutes during which snow had begun to fall. Earlier and more heavily than forecasted.

Adam adjusted his seat to a more upright position and looked around, frowning. "Danni?" A low warning sounded in his voice.

"Yes."

"The light is fading." He glanced at his watch. "And it's snowing."

"Yes. It's nothing the Range Rover can't handle." But she didn't like it all the same.

"And we still appear to be going up into the mountains."

"Ahh, yes, so it would seem."

"So it would seem?"

She didn't like the heavy sarcasm or the annoyance underlying his words.

"Why are we still going up?"

"Because…"

He waited—far too silently—for her to finish her explanation.

"Because that's how we get to the chalet, and now we're not so very far from it."

"The Marconi chalet?"

"You keep repeating my words."

"In an attempt to see if they make any more sense when it's not your mouth they're coming out of. Sadly, they don't. And you're going to have to explain."

"You fell asleep."

"I'm aware of that."

"And you looked so tired."

"Danni."

She couldn't ignore the warning in his tone. "And there really wasn't anywhere to turn around."

"For the last hour there's been nowhere?"

She didn't answer.

"Turn around. Now."

"I don't think it's a very good idea." They were only twenty-five minutes from the chalet.

"Clearly you don't think it's a good idea. But that doesn't concern me. What concerns me is getting back to the palace. Tonight. So that I can sleep the night in my own bed and do the things I'm supposed to be doing tomorrow." His voice was lethally quiet.

"I thought that you'd appreciate the enforced break. I thought you could use it."

"You thought wrong."

"Adam, I—"

A jolt shook the car. It shuddered and pulled to the right and at the same time an alarm sounded on the dashboard computer. All three things told her the same thing. The very last thing she wanted to happen.

A flat tire.

She pulled off to the side of the road. For a moment she sat there not daring to look at Adam. She held the wheel. "This will just take a couple of minutes. And then we'll be back on the road." She'd have it changed quicker than another vehicle could get here for assistance or to pick up Adam. She radioed in her intentions and got out.

By the time she reached the back of the car, he was already there, pushing his arms into a down jacket. "What are you doing?" She hitched up her own jacket onto her shoulders.

"I'm going to change the wheel." He spoke in a tone that indicated he would tolerate no disagreement.

She disagreed anyway. "No, you're not. I'm the driver. I'm going to change it. That's what I'm here for." Danni opened the back.

"You're here to drive me where I want to go and you weren't doing that."

"That's different."

"I'm not going to get into an argument with you." He spoke gently but implacably. "This is my car. I'm going to change the wheel." Adam reached in front of her and lifted out the spare tire.

"If I was a man, would you insist on changing it?" She grabbed the jack and the wrench and followed him to the wheel that sat heavily on its rim.

Adam set the tire down. "If you were your father I would."

Danni put the jack beside it and turned to him. She knew, and didn't like, the obstinate look in his eyes. "And he'd be just as insulted as I am."

"Deal with it. I'm not going to stand by and watch while you change the tire. What do you take me for?"

He stepped toward the jack and she insinuated herself into the sliver of space between him and the car, blocking his way.

"But you expect me to stand by and watch you? This is my job, Adam. It's what I'm here for."

"What you're here for is completely separate." He sidestepped but she moved with him.

"Not separate, because, in case you've forgotten, I drove you here. Your Highness." The title was supposed to remind him of their respective roles. It was also intended to let him know how irritated she was with him right now.

Snowflakes drifted between them. "Looks like you just solved our problem. I warned you what would happen if you called me Your Highness. You're fired. Which means you're not my driver, so stand aside."

Her temper flared. "You can't fire me without written warning." She had no idea if that restriction held true for the palace, a world that operated with its own rules. She only hoped Adam didn't know either—terms of employment for staff not being a major diplomatic concern. "So, as far as I'm concerned," she pressed on, "I'm still your driver and I'm going to change the wheel."

"No. You're not my driver and you're not going to change the wheel." He stepped closer, intimidating her with his size and his very nearness. Another inch and they'd be touching. She looked up and met the obstinate light in his eyes with what she hoped was its equal in hers. His breath mingled with hers. His warmth surrounded her. And a very different kind of warmth leaped deep within her. Her heart beat faster, her breath grew shallower. It took her a moment to register and recognize the sensation.

Desire. Need.

No. This couldn't be happening. Not with Adam. It was just the proximity. It was his very maleness, it was the insular life she led, lately devoid of male relationships that weren't purely about camaraderie.

The light in his eyes changed and darkened, the anger and stubbornness replaced by something she couldn't name. Time hung suspended. Slowly, he lowered his head. She breathed in his scent, and without meaning to, moistened her lips and swallowed. He was going to kiss her, and she shouldn't want it.

But she did.

In a single deft movement he slid his hands beneath her armpits, picked her up and set her to one side.

He smiled. Then dusted off his hands. Victorious. Satisfied with his win. Damn him.

It took seconds for her equilibrium to return, for her to get past the fact that she'd thought of Adam that way, and not just in some dim imagining, but with him right here where she could have, and almost had, reached for him. Because he was right there. She'd ached to know the taste of his lips on hers. It had seemed imperative.

And he had seen her thoughts and shunned her.

He crouched beside the wheel, positioned the jack and reached for the wrench, relegating Danni to the position of observer or at best support crew unless she wanted to tackle him out of the way. Which would get her precisely nowhere. She was left alternating between mortification at her reaction to him, and frustration at the fact that he'd so easily brushed her aside both as his driver and as a woman.

"If you fire me you'll have to drive yourself home. You'll lose all that time you could have spent working."

"With pleasure," he said, sounding as though he meant it. "At least I'll know I'll get where I want to go."

"You'll have to help yourself with your dating issues. Help yourself unwind and lighten up."

He raised his eyebrows and looked about them. "If this is your idea of helping me unwind, I can live without it."

He had a point. All she'd succeeded in achieving was to make matters worse.

Adam set to work on the wheel and Danni stood to the side and watched him. Snow dusted his head and shoulders. Petty as she knew it was, she silently tried to find fault with even the tiniest detail of how he changed the tire. He gave her no opportunity.

Usually she found strength and competence attractive. In Adam, now, coming after everything else, these traits were irrationally annoying. As he set the old tire on the ground she reached for it.

"Leave it," he said. "I'll get it when I'm done."

It sounded like an order. She ignored him, and to the sound of his sigh, wheeled it to the back of the car.

Sacked. She'd been sacked. Again. That was three times now.

If they were no longer employer and employee and they weren't friends, then what were they? Two ac-

quaintances temporarily stranded on the side of the
road as the snow began to fall more heavily. Everything
was too unpredictable. Including Adam.

Maybe she should have expected his annoyance
at her decision to override his request, but she hadn't
expected his obstinacy over changing the wheel, and
never could she have predicted that flash of awareness
that passed between them as they'd faced off. Out of everything, that bothered her the most. The sudden fierce-
ness of it had come out of nowhere.

No traffic passed by on the road. She walked back
and continued watching, trying to figure him out.
Adam was older, though not that much older; it had
just always seemed that way. But because of that and,
more importantly, their respective positions, he was un-
touchable. He was also supposed to be imperturbable,
safe and predictable, a touch on the staid side, considered and considerate, dependable. Anything listed in
the thesaurus under *safe* would do to describe him.
That's who he was.

Until now.

And if Adam wasn't being Adam, it turned her world
upside down.

She tucked her gloved hands beneath her arms and
bounced on her toes, trying to keep warm.

He lowered the car back to the ground and began
giving the wheel nuts a final tightening. "Get back in
the car. You're cold."

"I'm fine." She crouched beside him and reached for
the jack.

He glanced at her steadily. "Anyone ever tell you that
you're stubborn?"

"A lot of people as it happens, but it's a bit rich coming from you."

"Insolent?"

"I might give you that one."

He shook his head. "Provoking?"

"No more than you."

He stood. "Exasperating?"

She stood too, glaring up at him. "Pot and kettle."

Adam looked skyward, as though seeking help from the gray and darkening sky, before his eyes met hers again. Apparently he hadn't found the help he sought because frustration tightened his features.

And there it was again, that something else in his gaze. That something that did ridiculous things to her insides, made the world seem to tilt. She studied him, trying to hide her reaction and trying to figure out what it was that had changed. If she could pinpoint it, she could deal with it.

"Way more than me," he insisted, incredulous.

"No, because I—"

His hand snaked out, cupped the back of her head and drew her to him.

Adam's lips covered hers, stealing her words, replacing them with the taste of him, overwhelming her with the feel of him, the exquisite heat of his mouth against her cold skin, and the answering heat it ignited within her. He coaxed and dominated and she gave back and gave in, welcoming and returning his fervor.

This was what she'd wanted.

He was what she'd wanted.

Danni slid her arms around him, held him and angled her head, allowing him to deepen the kiss. Allowing him to draw her deeper under his spell. She welcomed the erotic invasion of his tongue. And the flames within her leaped higher as though he'd touched a match to gasoline.

The flash point of her response told her how much more she'd wanted this than she'd ever admitted. She lost herself in sensation. Enthralled, enraptured, ensnared.

In seconds he had her backed against the car, his hands cold and thrilling against her jaw. A counterpoint to the heat of his mouth. His fingers threaded into her hair. Fierce, possessive. His body pressed against hers and she arched into it, breasts to chest, hips to hips. Meeting and matching him. Governed by hunger. Slave to sensation. He was everything she wanted and more and he was everything she'd thought—almost hoped— he wasn't. Cool reserve replaced by searing passion.

He kissed her as though starved for her and awakened the same hunger within her.

Danni groaned, weakened and empowered, aflame.

Abruptly, he broke the kiss and drew back. His eyes, passion-glazed, met hers, and she watched as shock and regret replaced that passion. He snatched his hands from her head as though burned and clenched them into fists at his side.

A terrible silence welled.

Her frantic heartbeat slowed and she fought to calm her breathing. Adam swallowed. "Danni, I—"

"Don't." She turned away from him and picked up the jack and the wrench and strode to the back of the car. She couldn't bear to hear him apologize, to voice the regret written so clearly on his face. She didn't want to hear the word *mistake* from his lips.

Gritting her teeth, she stowed the tools in the back,

mortified by her untutored and revealing response to him. And despite everything she knew, all the things about Adam that would make it impossible for him to want her, or let himself want her, she waited, hoping against hope, that he would speak—not words of regret but something else.

But she could wait only so long.

In silence, Danni headed for the driver's door. Since protocol had clearly been abandoned and left twitching in the snow, she was going to make sure she was the one behind the wheel. It was the only chance she had of control. It would remind them both of who they each were.

He got in beside her, bringing strained silence with him.

There were no guidelines for this scenario.

Danni started the car and took a deep breath as she looked out into the near darkness and the now heavily falling snow. Just as Adam was remembering who he was, she had to remember her role, too. This was not the weather to be driving back in. Visibility would be almost non-existent and the road would be icy and soon snow-covered. Common sense, much as it pained her, had to prevail. She wanted nothing more than for this to be over. She was no coward, but she wanted to run and hide. Instead she took a deep breath and said, "I don't think we should head back to the palace this evening."

Six

Adam glanced at Danni sitting stoically behind the wheel, all her attention focused ahead. The atmosphere inside the car was more frigid than outside, and it wasn't because of the snow coating her hair and shoulders. A new tension tightened her jaw that had nothing to do with the deteriorating driving conditions and everything to do with that kiss.

She'd smelled of pine and snow and tasted of the mints she kept in the car, and for a second she had melded with him, her lithe body pressing into his even through the barrier of their clothing. He'd felt her surprise. He'd caught her reciprocated desire. As surprising for her as it had been for him. And for a moment nothing else had mattered.

She had come alive in his arms, fire and light. But

perhaps that was just Danni. She probably made love that way. His groan almost escaped out loud.

He had to stop remembering and reliving the kiss.

He'd messed up. Royally. And he had to make it right. He had to find a way to get things back to the way they were before he'd kissed her.

The kiss that should never ever have happened. The kiss that, in the moment, had seemed like the only right thing in the world. The kiss that had wrenched control from him and plunged him into a place where there was no thought, only sensation and desire.

But as he watched the snow falling outside he knew they had a more immediate issue to sort out first. "How far are we from the chalet?" he asked, his question more brusque than he'd intended. The control was difficult to reclaim. Even now traces of the consuming need lingered, pulsing through him, refusing to be suppressed.

But she was Danni and he would not let himself want her.

The kiss, the desire, was an aberration.

"Twenty-five minutes," she said quietly, pressing her lips together as soon as she'd spoken.

Those lips. The compulsion to taste her had overwhelmed him. The feeble justification flitting into his mind, that, as of a few minutes ago, she was no longer officially his driver had seemed a valid excuse. And stopping that kiss had been one of the hardest things he'd ever done. Only her groan of pure desire had cut through the fog of passion, allowing a moment of sanity.

Sweet, sassy Danni kissed like a dream. The most erotic of dreams. The way she'd responded, the way her

mouth had fit his, the feel of her body against his—all
had felt…perfect. All had promised forbidden pleasure.

It was afterward that regret had surged in. Once that
last shred of sanity had warned him to end the kiss, he'd
seen the shock in her eyes and realized what he'd done,
the boundaries he'd trampled over, the very wrongness
of kissing Danni, no matter how right it had felt.

His responsibility, much as she'd disagree, was to
protect her, not to claim her, to assault and insult her.
"Let's go to the chalet." Going to the chalet was the
best option given the deteriorating weather, though it
carried its own risks being alone with her there. But if
he kept duty to the forefront, perhaps it offered him a
glimmer of a chance to make it right with her. To get
things between them back to a place that was as close
to normal as possible. Because otherwise once they got
to the palace, they would go their separate ways and
he would lose her—their relationship irreparably dam-
aged. Because of him.

He studied her profile, searching for words. He was
reputed to be diplomatic. It was failing him now. Had
failed him already because that talent ought to have
stopped him from getting into this situation in the first
place.

He always thought before he acted or spoke.

Always.

Until that moment. And it was all to do with Danni.
She stirred him up in ways he couldn't like. She made
him forget to think.

"Danni—"

"I don't want to hear it, Adam."

She had to. They had to clear the air. "It was an accident."

"What, you slipped and fell and your lips landed on mine?" She shook her head and a slight smile touched her lips.

"I—"

"Just don't. I know everything you're going to say and you don't have to. It shouldn't have happened. We both know that. You're going to try to take all the blame yourself, as though it had nothing to do with me. As though I hadn't wanted it, too. Just once. Just to know. You're going to say we should forget it happened, put it behind us and move forward."

He wanted to refute her words. But she'd gotten it right.

"So let's do that," she said. "We'll forget it." She clenched her jaw and glared at the road ahead.

One of the things they had in common was that neither of them liked to admit an injury or a weakness. Perhaps that would work in their favor here. "Do you really think it's possible? That was no ordinary kiss." His head still spun, the blood still surged in his veins.

"I'll give you that, it wasn't ordinary. Far from it. And I should probably retract my implication after your date with Clara that there must be something wrong with your technique. Because clearly there's not. But we can leave it at that."

"Can we?" It was the right thing to do, the only way forward.

"Of course we can. It was a heat-of-the-moment mistake and that moment has passed. It was one minute out of all the years we've known each other. The years should count for more than the minute, don't you think?"

"Yes."

"So, if you're going to apologize for anything it should be for sacking me."

"You called me Your Highness."

"You were being a pompous ass."

"Good thing you're already fired."

She grinned, and that small flash of smile lifted a weight from him.

"That's three times now you've sacked me. Each time unjustified."

"You made me spill coffee on my shirt."

"I didn't want to hit the pothole."

The truth had nothing to do with the coffee and everything to do with the look that had passed between them when he'd taken off his shirt. The surge of desire he'd felt for her. She'd only been twenty-one, and his friend, and he hadn't wanted to feel that for her. But he'd stepped away from the friendship anyway. And he'd missed it. Not often, but sometimes in the quiet moments he thought of her.

"So can we talk about something else? Please?"

If she was prepared to try, if she was prepared to move on, then he could, too. "Tell me about the Grand Prix."

"Thank you." She sighed her relief, and filled him in on the latest developments in bringing a Grand Prix to San Philippe. And while at first there was an obvious strain to her words, over time, as they talked, it really did become easier, a little more natural. Neither of them had forgotten the kiss, but the conversation, the finding of common neutral ground, gave him hope that the damage wasn't irreversible.

After ten minutes their headlights picked out a sign through the swirling snow. It advertised an inn he didn't remember seeing before. He glanced at Danni. She wore driving gloves but he was certain that if he could see her hands, her grip would be white-knuckled. And they had another fifteen minutes of driving to go, at least, possibly longer given the speed with which conditions were deteriorating. "Let's try here."

"But—" Her argument died on her lips and she did as he suggested.

She stopped beneath the portico in front of the Austrian-style chalet. It was smaller by far than the Marconi chalet but offered respite from the driving and shelter from the weather. That was all they needed. That and somewhere he could put some space between them.

"I'll go in and check that they have rooms," she said, in the guise of chauffeur not friend, as she reached for her door. And maybe chauffeur was safer.

His hand on her arm—a new but hardly significant breach of protocol given what had already happened—stilled her before she could open her door. Despite the thaw of the last ten minutes, he at least, couldn't move on without actually apologizing.

She turned back but only enough that she could look straight ahead through the windshield. "Don't," she said, reading what was on his mind. "It never happened. We're moving on."

A sharp tapping on her window startled them both. They turned to see a hulk of a man blocking the window, his face shrouded by the hood of his coat. Danni glanced at Adam and waited for his nod before lowering her window.

"You finally made it," the man shouted against the gusting wind. "Drive around to the side. I'll open the garage door." Without waiting for a response he disappeared back inside.

Danni looked at Adam again, her eyebrows raised in inquiry, hesitation in her gaze, making it his call. He knew he should be grateful that at least she was looking at him with something other than appalled horror. He nodded. "Let's go in."

"He must be expecting someone else."

"Well, he's got us. Drive round. Unless you have a better suggestion?"

She radioed their location to the palace and then eased the car around the side of the building and into the garage.

Their host stood waiting. He'd shed his coat but he looked no less of a bear of a man than he had outside. Tall and broad, in need of a haircut and with a furrowed brow. The furrows eased as Danni and Adam got out of the car, and he smiled. "I was beginning to worry you might not make it tonight."

"We're not who you're expecting." Adam waited for recognition to dawn on the other man's face.

"That's okay. So long as you can cook."

From the corner of his eye he saw a flicker of a smile touch Danni's lips. Adam wasn't often expected to be able to cook when he arrived at an inn. "I know a couple of dishes but I have to admit, cooking's not my strong point. We were heading for a chalet further up the mountain—" he didn't say which one "—but saw your sign. And the weather's atrocious out there."

"Oh." The single word was disappointment itself. "You're not Simon?"

He shook his head. "Sadly, no."

"Well, you're here. And you can't go back out. But

the food's not going to be very good." A hint of an accent colored his words. "My name's Blake by the way. Your accidental host. Should have said that first. It's in the list of instructions in my notebook. But I keep forgetting them." He absently patted at his pockets. "I'm just looking after this place for a few days so it's all new to me and there are too many things to remember, too many proper ways and wrong ways of doing the simplest of things. They have some high-falutin' guests stay from time to time who apparently have the pickiest expectations. Everything has to be just so, and done in convoluted ways." His glance took them both in and a smile broke out. "I can tell you two aren't like that." The smile faded. "Are you?" he finished hopefully.

"Not at all," Adam said, grateful for their *accidental* host's warmth and rough charm. It covered and eased the tension. "I'm Adam and this is Danni," he said before Danni could say anything, because she'd taken a deep breath as though about to launch into an explanation. If Blake didn't know who he was, Adam was happy enough to keep it that way. Already the anonymity, when he'd been prepared for any number of different reactions, felt like one less issue to deal with.

"Come on inside. Can't have been pleasant driving in that. I'll get you a drink." Blake smiled. "That's the one instruction I never forget."

"I'll just get our bags," Danni said.

"Wouldn't hear of it. I'll get them." Blake was at the back of the car retrieving their bags before either of them had time to object. "Here, you take this one." Blake passed Danni's bag to Adam. He saw her mortification and shook his head. She didn't like him carrying her bag. But unless she wanted to fight him for it—and for a moment it looked as though she might—she'd just have to deal with it.

"What do you mean by accidental host?" he asked Blake, trying to deflect her attention.

"Crikey."

That one word told him that Blake was, as he'd suspected, Australian. Danni's smile grew.

"You wouldn't believe the rotten string of luck that's led to me being alone here," he said as he crossed the garage. "The place is owned by my sister-in-law. It's been in her family for years. She's been coping on her own these last two years since my brother died and has turned it into an inn. I was only coming over for a holiday and to give her a hand when Sabrina—"

He reached an internal door and looked back. "Nah. You don't want to know all that. All you need to know is that people have been breaking their legs and having babies when they shouldn't, and now getting waylaid by weather, so you've got me."

He led them up a flight of stairs. "We don't have any guests booked in for a couple days. I was expecting the new chef and his wife. The chef was a friend of my brother's. But I have a suspicion that if he was a friend of Jake's—and yes, I know, *Blake and Jake*, what were my parents thinking?" He barely paused for breath but his voice had a surprisingly melodic quality to it that was easy to listen to and Adam tried to focus on that rather than Danni, and the sway of her hips, as she walked up the stairs ahead of him.

Blake reached the top, set Adam's case down and turned to wait for them. "Anyway, if he's a friend of Jake's, chances are he's found himself a tavern and holed up there. And if I'm right and he has found a tavern, there's no telling when we'll see him, regardless of what the weather does. The useless—"

Blake stopped himself and grinned as Danni and Adam halted in front of him. It was a surprisingly sheepish expression for such a big man. He reached to take Danni's case from Adam. "You should know that at the very top of the list of the instructions Sabrina left for me was to not talk too much. And never ever to swear in front of guests. Written in red. Because I wasn't supposed to deal with the public, really. Simon's wife's going to do that. So, let's just get that drink I talked about. And don't worry, there'll be dinner for tonight and it'll will be warm and tasty if not fancy." He glanced from the cases at his feet to another set of stairs. "I'll take these up to your room in a jiffy."

"Rooms." Adam said with an emphasis on the *s*. "We'll need two." He said it before Danni had to. Though for a second the thought of sharing a room—a bed—with her, had stirred something fierce within him, something that had catapulted his mind back to when he was kissing her.

The kiss and the associated sensations had imprinted on him and he didn't think it was going to be possible to erase them. They would, he was certain, haunt him for a long time to come.

"Two?" Blake looked between them, frowning.

"That's not a problem, is it?"

"No," he said drawing the word out. "But seeing as I was expecting the chef and his wife, I only have one room ready. But it won't take me long to sort out. I'll do it while you're drinking your mulled wine. You will have a glass of mulled wine, won't you?" He trained a look of earnest concern on them. "I have some ready."

"We'd love to, thanks," Danni said with a smile that wiped the concern from Blake's face.

He showed them into a cavernous living room with high wooden-beamed ceilings and a roaring fire in a stone hearth. "You stay by the fire. I'll be back in two shakes of a lamb's tail."

Danni looked from Blake's departing back to Adam. "I haven't apologized for overriding your request to go back to the palace. For us ending up here."

And if she hadn't done that he wouldn't have kissed her and they wouldn't be in this mess. "It's okay. I appreciate your reasoning." He knew she'd done it for him because she'd thought he needed to take some time for himself.

"We don't have to stay here if it doesn't suit you."

"What do you mean?"

She looked around the room. "This is nice but it isn't going to be what you're used to, especially with no staff. I can get us to the Marconi chalet if you'd like."

"Okay, so now I am annoyed. What do you take me for, Danni? *This isn't what I'm used to.* You know I served in the military. I had plenty of accommodations during my time that were far less salubrious than this. Almost all of it, in fact."

"I know but…"

"I thought you were one of the few people who saw beyond the title."

"I do."

"Yet you think I'd rather send us both back out into that weather, not to mention insulting Blake, for the sake of what? A higher thread count? Someone to open doors?"

"A better meal," she suggested.

"I don't care about the food."

She looked away. "You're right. I know you're not like that." Had his kiss driven such a wedge between them that she couldn't even meet his gaze?

Another thought occurred to him. "You don't have a problem with Blake?"

"Me? No." She looked as horrified as he'd been when she'd suggested he might not consider this place up to his usual standard. But then a sudden merriment flashed in her eyes as she added, "He's gorgeous, mate."

Relief flooded through him. That was the Danni he remembered.

Her grin faded too soon. "We should tell him who you are."

Which in turn dimmed his own enjoyment in her response. "Why?"

"Because he has a right to know."

"Can you imagine what that will do to him? He's already flustered."

"But—"

"He doesn't need to know."

"Is that an order?" She raised one eyebrow.

Why did she always have to challenge and question him? He'd never figured it out. Never figured *her* out. "I don't give you orders, Danni. I never have. And not just because you wouldn't have followed them."

She did a funny little head tilt that he took to be grudging acknowledgment of the truth. "But sometimes your requests do sound a lot like orders."

He shrugged. That was his acknowledgment that

maybe there was also an element of truth in what she said. He'd learned to be careful about how he expressed his thoughts and wishes because they could be taken too seriously. But it also meant that if he wanted something done, a subtle remark was usually enough to see it accomplished.

Blake came back in carrying two cinnamon-scented glasses of mulled wine. "Here, get these down you and I'll sort out your other room. That is, if you're sure you don't want to share."

"We're sure," they said in unison.

They watched him go and Danni laughed. "I'd bet my life's savings that no one's ever handed you a drink and told you to 'get it down you' before."

"Your savings are safe." Adam raised his glass to her and looked about the room. His gaze took in an antique chess set positioned between two armchairs. The pieces set up for a game. "Do you want to play?" Anything to keep her distracted, to pull things back to where they ought to be between them.

She looked from the board to him. "I've barely played since the last time with you."

"Me neither."

"Are you lying?" she asked, suspicion narrowing her eyes.

"I might have played a time or two. What about you?"

Her lips twitched. "A time or two."

They could move on. He knew it. She'd never been one to hold grudges, preferring to live in the present.

"I'm not sure that now's the best time to get back into it though, because in all our matches that summer and the few afterward, I never won a game off you."

"I wouldn't remember."

"You remember. You're too competitive not to. But that last time I had you in check twice."

"Once. And it only lasted until my next move when I put you in checkmate."

"It was twice and it took way more moves than one to make it checkmate. I almost had you."

"Prove it." He nodded at the set.

She hesitated.

"There's nothing else for us to do. Unless you want to talk about what happened before?"

"I'm white," she said with a false cheerfulness.

Adam waited for her to sit and watched as she touched and aligned each of the intricately carved pieces. "It's a beautiful set," she said, picking up a finely carved knight and turning it slowly.

"I'm guessing it's an original Staunton." He lifted his king and looked at its base. "Ebony and boxwood made around the 1860s. And it's your move."

"I knew it would come to that," she muttered. She opened with her king's pawn. "The trouble is you taught me. You know how I play because it's how you taught me to play. It seems like an unfair advantage."

"Which means you know how I think and play, too. But you quickly developed your own strategies. Unconventional but occasionally effective."

She shook her head. "The difference now is I'm not going to let your gamesmanship put me off."

"Gamesmanship?" He feigned outrage. That had been one of the things he'd enjoyed about playing with her. The way she tried to match wits with him verbally as well as strategically.

"Gee, Danni. Are you sure you want to do that?" She

mimicked him. "'Are you sure you've thought through all the avenues? The obvious move isn't always the best one.' You turned me round in circles, like that labyrinth at the palace."

"I never gave you bad advice. Besides, you were more than capable of thinking your way out of it. And you always liked the labyrinth."

"You were five years older than me."

"You wanted to play." He mirrored her move.

"I always thought I could beat you—one day. And then we stopped playing, just as I was getting better and coming close to matching you."

"I was letting you think you were coming close because, like you said, I had five years on you. It was only fair to give you a chance."

"Says the man who taught me the French proverb, *you cannot play chess if you are kindhearted.* You weren't *letting* me come close to winning. I was doing that on my own. In fact that's probably why you stopped playing with me."

"And of course it had nothing to do with me going back to boarding school."

"That might have been a factor." She grinned.

"And if we're talking sayings, I lost count of how many times you reminded me that after the game, the king and the pawn go back in the same box."

"Still true."

And he was just as grateful now as he had been then that she thought that way. He paused with his hand on a knight. "Those chess games helped me get through that vacation."

"Only because winning makes you happy. Don't expect it tonight." Challenge and anticipation lit her eyes.

And the same sensations stirred within him. "Okay, Kasparov. Show me what you've got. But I'm thinking you're still going to make me a happy man." He hadn't intended the double entendre. But he could see by the way her eyes widened before she looked quickly back at the board that she'd read more into those words than he'd intended. And he too had thought more than he ought as soon as they were out of his mouth. In that fleeting instant he'd thought of ways Danni might make him happy and of ways he might please her, and of how she would look in the throes of pleasure. Forbidden thoughts. He had to stop them.

And he had to get his head into the game or she'd beat him. She made her next move and they played in the silence of concentration for fifteen minutes until Blake came back.

"Glad to see that being used." He nodded at the chess set. "It belonged to my grandfather. Only Jake ever played and even then not much." He stood a short distance away, his hands behind his back, and surveyed the board. "Who's winning?"

Danni met Adam's gaze then looked at Blake. "Hard to say at this point." Adam agreed with her assessment. Already she'd surprised him a couple of times. He was going to have to work for a win.

"Do you want to finish the game before I show you up to your rooms?"

Adam looked at Danni whose attention was back on the board, her hand hovering over her bishop. "This game may not finish anytime soon."

Blake shook his head. "That's the trouble with

chess," he grumbled. "Takes too long and you can't even tell who's winning."

Danni made her move and then with one last look at the board, stood and smiled at their host. Blake gestured to the door. "It took me a while to find everything. But I think I've done it right. Ticked off everything on the list anyway." The crinkling of paper sounded as he patted his pocket. "I'll show you up now and then fix your dinner. Like I said, it won't be fancy, but it'll be tasty and there'll be plenty of it. I'm more used to cooking for a shearing gang than couples on vacation. I hope you're hungry."

"I could eat a horse?" Adam said tentatively.

Clearly the right answer. Blake clapped him forcefully on the back. "That's what I like to hear," he said as he led the way up the stairs. "I've put Danni in here." He opened a door to a bedroom with a canopied four-poster bed in the center draped in a white linen coverlet, with a heart-shaped chocolate wrapped in red foil on the pillow. "It's the best room," he said proudly.

"Bathroom's over there," Blake pointed to a far door and then walked to another. "This is the adjoining door. It can be locked from either side. Or not." The man clearly thought there was something going on between them. Or that there would be soon. An idea that teased at Adam's senses no matter how he tried to repress it. But repress it he had to. There could be nothing between the two of them for a whole host of reasons. Her age and the fact that he was looking for a wife being the first two that came to mind. A wife to stand at his side now and when the time came for him to fill his father's shoes as monarch of the country. A role that wouldn't suit the adventure-loving Danni and one which he couldn't imagine her suiting in return. He knew what he needed in a partner—he had his list.

So, anything with Danni, as tempting and insistent as the idea suddenly was, would be wrong because it wouldn't be fair to her. And would ruin a relationship that he was only now coming to properly value.

She was out-of-bounds.

The room revealed by the opened door was similar though smaller than the one they stood in. The bed was a standard bed, the covers were somewhat rumpled in a testament to Blake's bed-making skills. Though here too in the center of the pillow sat a foil-wrapped chocolate.

Danni looked at him, her narrowed gaze revealing her discomfort. He was assuming the discomfort was over the disparity in their rooms rather than the proximity. He only wished he could say the same for himself. He'd never have thought having Danni St. Claire so close could be disconcerting, but he knew without a shadow of a doubt that he'd be lying in bed tonight and thinking about her on the other side of that door.

That kiss had a lot to answer for. *He* had lot to answer for. And she hadn't let him apologize for it.

Then again, maybe he'd kissed her just to stop her arguing.

No. Not true.

He'd kissed her because he'd suddenly wanted to. Needed to so badly that he hadn't been able not to. And there was a part of him, a traitorous rebellious part, that couldn't regret it, that triumphed in it.

Worst of all was the fact that she'd responded. Un-equivocally. An encouragement he would have been much better off without. That instantaneous connection and heat had been like no other kiss.

Usually he made quick irrevocable decisions and seldom revisited them, seldom regretted them. This confusion, the indecision and second-guessing that assailed him was uncharted and disturbing territory.

Danni opened her mouth to protest over the room arrangement. He silenced her with a hand on her shoulder. "These look terrific," he said. "Thank you."

"I knew you'd appreciate them. Sabrina knows how to do things nicely." Their host kept talking, oblivious to the sensation rioting through Adam, and all because of the feel of her slender shoulder. "And those chocolates," Blake pointed to the pillow, "are delicious. Just had one when I was making your bed. I couldn't help it." He clapped his hands together. "So, dinner now?"

"Can you give us fifteen minutes, please?" Danni asked, stepping away from Adam's side.

"That's even better. Of course you'll be wanting a bit of private time. And I'll be able to make sure it's all properly ready and hot. Sing out if you need anything. Just come down when you're ready."

As soon as Blake left, Danni turned to Adam, her gaze earnest. He missed the feel of her close to him.

"We're swapping rooms," she said as she started for her suitcase.

Adam blocked her way. "No. We're not."

"Yes. We are." She sidestepped.

He matched her, again blocking her way with his body. "No. We're not. And that *is* an order."

"Ha. Remember what you said about me not being likely to follow your orders. You were right. My room's twice the size of yours. I wouldn't be able to sleep in it. You're the one who's a prince."

"You're only here because of me. It's very right. All it is is a bed to sleep in anyway." And no matter which bed he was in he wouldn't be getting much sleep. Not with her so close. "I'll bet you've always wanted to sleep in a four-poster bed."

Her irrepressible grin lifted one side of her mouth. "Actually, when I was younger my fantasies ran more to a racing car bed."

"But what about now? Where do your fantasies run to now?" His fantasies suddenly included her laughing lips.

They were standing close. He could see flecks of gold in her eyes. He could see the tips of her teeth revealed by her parted lips. He took a step back. "I'm sorry. That was inappropriate and not something I need to know." Her mouth closed and she bit her lip, drawing attention to its soft fullness.

He should turn and go, but he stood there staring at her, wanting her. And he could see the mirror of his wanting in her eyes.

Hope twined with desire inside him. *Hope* that she felt something of what he did, and *desire* for her, here and now. He didn't want either. He *shouldn't* want either. And together they were a fearsome combination.

Where was her outrage over his earlier kiss? The overstepping of bounds, the abuse of power? He'd settle for sympathy and a gentle admonishment that she didn't think of him that way, or even for her to laugh in his face. He could deal with any of those. Anything to remind him that the sudden attraction laying siege to him was one-sided and had to be vanquished, that kissing her could never be allowed to happen again. Because that was what was right and safe.

But it wasn't one-sided. He could see that now. It hadn't been just him in that kiss. The attraction simmered between them.

He should step away, not want to pull her closer. Her lips had a newfound power over him. He wanted, so much that it was a need, to kiss her again.

He looked away from her—her eyes, her lips, her hair, her feminine curves, everything that tempted him—so that he could think clearly. But instead he saw that big four-poster bed and pictured Danni in it. With him.

It was insanity. Lust—that's all it was—was gaining the upper hand.

He was alone here with Danni, when he'd planned a weekend with no work, no distractions, so now he was fixating on her. If his date, Claudia—he struggled to remember her name—was here that wouldn't be happening. Although he could scarcely remember what Claudia looked like. She was ostensibly a beauty but she had none of Danni's spirit and sass. And everything going on in his head was just plain wrong and he couldn't, wouldn't allow it.

Even if he'd correctly interpreted the way she'd melted into him. Even if she hadn't wanted him to stop that kiss.

His thoughts refused to be suppressed.

Danni's expression as she watched him turned thoughtful. She knew he was battling with himself. And as that realization registered, the light in her eyes changed, desire shone through. The desire that had sprung to life between them, more powerful for being mutual and forbidden. The hunger for her gnawing at him almost undid him. He could pull her to him now....

He might not have control over his thoughts or his desires but he still had control over his actions and he removed his hand from her shoulder and turned away from her.

It felt like the hardest thing he'd ever done.

He crossed the room, putting necessary distance between them. "We need to talk about what's happening here. We're alone together for the first time and I don't know how or why, but somehow it's changing things. But not everything. And what remains constant is the fact that anything between us would be wrong. It's not that I don't want...it's just all kinds of wrong."

"You think I don't know that? That you're stuck here without your duties to occupy you, or the woman who should have been here, so you're focusing on me. A convenient substitute."

She waited for him to disagree. "Yes," he said. Though it wasn't that. Not by a long shot. This attraction to her was anything but convenient. Danni was all the things that were missing in his life, things she'd pointed out, spontaneity, honesty, and this felt like his last chance to grab them. But, and it kept coming back to this, it would be wrong. Unfair to her when she deserved so much more. "So let's just go to dinner. And we are not swapping rooms." He spoke as coldly as he could. "Tomorrow we're going home. Things will be back to normal."

He crossed to the door, each step away from her heavy and determined, as though he was fighting gravity.

"Adam?"

He shouldn't respond, but he turned. And she was right there. Her hands went to his head and pulled him down and she rose up on her toes and kissed him. A kiss of contradictions. Sweet and hard. A kiss that challenged and dared, and the press of her lips to his, of her body against his, the taste of her, filled him with fire.

The kiss undid all of his resolutions, weakened him. She took and she gave and left him mindless of anything other than her.

Then she broke the kiss and strode away.

Relief and regret tore through him as he sagged against the wall.

Seven

Danni woke to a soft tapping on the door. She had no idea what time it was other than early. So she rolled over and ignored it. The tapping grew louder. "I'm fine. I don't need anything." Except maybe a glass of water but she could get that for herself.

Blake had knocked just like that last night as she was about to get into bed because he'd forgotten to check that her bathroom had everything it ought to. And although those few minutes of Blake's garrulous company after the strained torture of dinner with Adam had been a blessing, she didn't want to see him, or anybody, right now.

Adam had been polite during their meal. Too polite. And charming. Too charming. There had been nothing real or honest about their conversation. The manners and the charm masked a remoteness that seemed impossible to bridge.

She'd all but told him that she wanted him. And he'd turned her down. Supposedly hell had no fury like a woman scorned, but she wasn't feeling scorn so much as mortification.

A chasm had opened up between them and it was of her making. She'd kissed him and he'd let her walk away. He hadn't mentioned the kiss during dinner. Not once.

She'd hoped that his gentle but undeniable rebuff would quell the insane one-sided lust that had sprung from nothing and nowhere in the space of a few days. But apparently insane lust didn't work that way. And she was still hankering, twisted up on the inside with wanting him.

She'd had wine with dinner in her desperation to forget. Not much, but usually she drank nothing. The wine had given no consolation and no reprieve from her embarrassment.

He was Adam Marconi. Heir to the throne of San Philippe. She was the daughter of one of the palace drivers. He'd known her since she was five. He didn't even think of her as a woman. If only there was a way to get through this day without seeing him.

"Danni?"

Her breath caught in her chest and every muscle tensed. It wasn't Blake at the door. It was Adam. And the tapping hadn't been at the main door to her room but at the adjoining door.

"Danni? I'm coming in."

Danni burrowed farther beneath the covers. "What do you want?" She knew there was no way of completely avoiding seeing him today but surely it didn't have to start now.

He opened the door enough that he could look into the room, his gaze somewhere on the wall above her head. He didn't so much as put a toe past the threshold. "We're going skiing. Did you bring gear?"

"Yes. I'm always prepared for anything, and I wasn't going to twiddle my thumbs while you were off skiing. But I thought we were going back to the palace today?"

He opened the door a little wider. "We're going skiing first. It snowed heavily overnight again and although it's stopped now, it'll be several hours before the roads have all been cleared. So we're stuck here for a while." He was clean shaven, his dark hair slightly damp. "Blake tells me there's a small ski field a five-minute walk from here. I thought we'd try it. It's got to be better than...being cooped up in here." He didn't add, *with her*. She didn't need the reminder of what she'd done last night. "Breakfast will be ready in fifteen minutes. Can you be ready?" His gaze lowered and tracked over her rumpled bed. Rumpled because she'd tossed and turned most of the night.

"Of course I can." He was sounding a degree or two warmer than he had last night, a little more like his usual self, as though he had put yesterday and last night behind him, as though he could pretend it had never happened. Relief washed through her. She couldn't forget what she had done, her madness. But perhaps they could get back to a place of...comfort between them. A place where they both pretended. She just had to show him that she could be normal. And if normal meant spending the morning on the slopes with him to prove herself, she could do it. Skiing would be the perfect distraction and a much better alternative to staying indoors alone and stewing.

* * *

The only sound in the still morning was the quiet crunch of their boots on the snow. Danni focused on the trail lightly trampled by the few people who'd come this way already this morning. Ahead, she could make out the next three orange-tipped trail markers before their path disappeared in a gap between the pines.

The chalet had a snowmobile but she'd only been half listening to Blake's convoluted explanation as to why it wasn't available this morning. But the walk, Blake had assured them though he hadn't done it himself, was short.

"It's beautiful," Danni said. The beauty, the serenity, helped give her perspective. Her turmoil was just that, hers. And not important. Or at least she knew that one day it would seem unimportant even if that day wasn't quite here yet.

"It is," Adam agreed easily, his step keeping pace with hers.

Breakfast with him had been marginally better than dinner. They were both valiantly pretending the kisses had never happened, both trying to act normally with each other. They were managing. Just. Like bad actors in a play. She could believe it if she forced herself to.

Through a gap between some pines, Danni glimpsed the rustic buildings of the ski field farther up the hill and guessed that Blake's five-minute estimation of the trip was optimistic. "I'll bet you don't usually have to walk to your ski fields lugging your own gear," she said. She tried for a teasing tone but guilt over the fact that it was her decisions that had put him in this predicament gnawed at her. If she hadn't ignored his wishes yesterday, none of this would have happened.

"Not usually, no." He glanced at her. "But I'll bet you don't, either."

"Good point. I guess not." She looked at the markers ahead. "You know, if we skip that next marker and head straight for the one beyond it, it'll be quicker. Some of the footprints already go this way." She headed in the direction she'd suggested, not waiting for Adam to agree. Because he wouldn't. He played by the book. He didn't take shortcuts.

"Why is it you have such a poor opinion of me?" He spoke across the few feet of snow that separated them.

She glanced at him, but with his hat and glasses in the way, too little of his face was visible to gauge how serious his question had been. "I don't."

"You do. You think I'm soft and spoiled and arrogant. Not to mention boring and uptight."

"I never said those things, especially not soft." She tried to remember what she might have ever said about him.

He laughed. Loud and deep. "But that's how you think of me."

His laughter was a relief and a balm. "You're a prince Adam. You've had a life of utter privilege. Apart from a few years in the military."

"You grew up on the palace grounds. You had a lot of those same privileges and, might I add, none of the responsibilities."

Danni said nothing. She couldn't totally agree with him but she also couldn't totally disagree with him.

"It helps you, doesn't it?" he said.

"It helps me what?"

"You prefer not to see me as a normal man. It wasn't

always like that. But I am normal and that's why I have to keep my distance."

She laughed but hers was a little forced. "You're not normal. Nothing about you is normal." She didn't want to hear whatever explanation he'd come up with for rejecting her. "You wouldn't know normal if it jumped up and bit you on the—"

He waited for her to finish but she held her tongue. Too late, but she held it anyway. "You see," he said. "You won't even use words you'd usually use because you're with me. And you used to not be like that. I know that's my fault and I need to fix it. I just don't know how."

If she'd changed it was because she did see him as a normal man now. One who might have needs, one who could fill needs she didn't want to own. She deviated a little farther off the visible path, wanting to put more space between them.

"Bit me where, Danni? Go on, finish your sentence."

There was too much of a challenge in his voice for her to refuse, too much of an assumption that she wouldn't. "Bit you on your fine royal ass."

He smiled. "Thank you. For that openness and for calling my ass fine."

The way those ski pants fit him, there was no doubt about that whatsoever. Not that she was going to admit it to him. "You can also be a royal pain in the ass."

"Again, thank you."

She laughed. "You were like this when Rafe used to tease you, too. Imperturbable, unfathomable. It was totally exasperating. We jumped off the groundsman's shed roof that time just to see how you'd react. You barely batted an eyelid."

"It used to drive him nuts."

"He has my sympathy."

"He always did."

There was something she couldn't quite grasp in his tone. "Meaning?"

"Nothing. But you two were quite the team when you were younger."

"United in tormenting you."

He nodded.

"We were doing you a favor." She looked across the few feet that separated them, trying to see how he'd take that assertion.

"I don't think I ever thanked you for it."

"There's no need for sarcasm." She hid her smile. "We kept you real, and grounded. Stopped your head from getting too full with all that rubbish you insisted on cramming into it."

"By rubbish you mean…?"

Danni paused. "Maybe it doesn't seem so much like rubbish now."

"So you mean my studies? Languages?"

She nodded. "Like Latin."

"You made me teach you some of it."

"I was young and impressionable."

"It may be a dead language but it lives on in other languages it forms the basis for—"

He caught her smiling and grinned back before he looked away, shaking his head.

"See, you just can't help yours—" She squawked as she stepped into a snow drift and sank down to her thighs. She tossed her skis and boots ahead of her and tried to work her way out. Adam stopped to watch her floundering. Finally she held out a hand to him.

He set his things down beside hers, took a few steps closer and looked at her outstretched hand. "Ah, so now I can be of service to you. Now I'm not so boring for preferring to follow the trail markers. And perhaps not quite so useless, hmm?" The light teasing in his voice was invigorating.

"I'm hoping not. But it's not anything you learned in Latin that I need from you now."

"Adsisto." Testing the snow he eased forward and reached for her hand.

"Gratia," she said as she accepted his clasp. He pulled her up and toward him. In two steps she stood pressed fully against him, and he steadied her with an arm around her back. And all the sensations, all the memories, came flooding back. Time stood still. His gaze dipped and flicked up again, then he blinked, long and slow, and stepped back. Away from her.

"Do you ski much?" he asked as the field came into view a couple silent minutes later. "I should have asked earlier. I just assumed."

"You assumed right." Her heartbeat had settled back to somewhere around normal. "I go whenever I get the chance." Even her voice sounded normal, revealing nothing of the breathless, and as it turned out pointless, anticipation she'd felt pressed against him. "I love skiing. The freedom, the speed, the exhilaration." She'd wanted his kiss, had almost been able to taste it. She'd learned nothing from last night.

"I guess that's why I assumed you did. Anything that involves speed and exhilaration and the risk of breaking your neck."

"You like it, too," she reminded him.

"Yes. I do," he agreed.

"I never thought we'd have anything in common. We're so different. Or at least you pretend you are."

"It's not me pretending I'm not like you. I freely admit who I am. It's you who's in denial. You're more like me than you want to admit."

"I'm nothing like you. You're royalty, you're a scholar, multilingual and let's face it, a bit of a geek."

"A geek? As in I like things like…chess?"

"Yes," she said slowly, seeing immediately where he was going with this, "but I only ever learned because we were both laid up that time, you with your leg and me with chicken pox. I was bored and had gone through all the other games and you'd gotten banned from everything electronic for crashing the palace network."

"The excuses won't work, Danni. Admit it, you enjoy chess."

"Yes," she admitted. "But that doesn't mean anything."

The Lord of the Rings. Adam had given her the books and insisted she read them prior to the first of the movie adaptations coming out. He'd re-read them at the same time and they'd had many lengthy discussion about them.

"Face it, Danni. Underneath the Action Woman exterior you're part geek, too. And it's not geeky but we have skiing in common."

She focused on the buildings ahead and the chairlifts stretching up the hill before them. "Yes, but—"

"And don't forget cars. You may not like who I am and what I do, but that doesn't mean you're not like me, that we don't have things in common."

She swallowed her shock. "I never said I don't like

who you are and what you do." He couldn't possibly think that. Could he?

"No?"

They reached the periphery of the clusters of skiers waiting for tickets or chairs. "No. I totally admire who you are and what you do. I always have. I can't imagine anyone better suited to it."

"I'm not sure that's a compliment."

"It is," she said quietly.

He stopped walking but because of his glasses she couldn't read what was in his eyes. He'd opened his mouth to say something when the sound of a sob caught their attention. Danni looked down to see a girl of about five or six looking woefully around, her eyes wide and panicked. She dropped to her knees in front of the child. "What are you looking for? Have you lost someone?"

The girl nodded, the rabbit ears on her ski hat bobbing. "I can't find my daddy." Her bottom lip and her voice trembled.

"That's okay," Danni said brightly, "because I know how to find lost daddies."

"Do you?"

"I sure do." She passed her skis to Adam.

"There's an information kiosk just over there," he said quietly to her.

She turned back to the girl. "Hold my hand and we'll go to that little building." She pointed to the kiosk, where a number of people were milling around. "They have a special place for lost fathers."

The girl put her gloved hand into Danni's. "What's your name?"

"Georgia."

"Come on then, Georgia. Let's go find your daddy. I'll bet he's really worried." Danni quietly prayed that Daddy had noticed the missing child and would also have gone to the kiosk.

Adam walked ahead of them, cutting a path through the crowd. At the kiosk he tapped on the shoulder of a tall man gesticulating wildly, who stopped and turned. Adam pointed out Danni and Georgia and the man came running. "Is that your daddy?" Danni asked the girl.

Georgia saw her father, said "Daddy," and promptly burst into tears. The man scooped up Georgia, enfolding her in a hug. "Are you okay, honey?"

Georgia nodded into her father's shoulder, her sobs subsiding. "The pretty lady knew how to find lost daddies."

He swung an arm around Danni and pulled her into a fierce embrace. "Thank you, thank you. I only turned around for a moment. And then she was gone." His voice was marginally steadier than his daughter's had been earlier.

"She's fine." Danni disentangled herself from father and daughter. "And a lovely girl. Enjoy your skiing." She wasn't even sure he heard, he was so busy hugging his daughter.

She turned to find Adam standing close by. "You handled that well," he said, admiration in his eyes.

"Thanks."

"Pretty lady."

"Enough with the sarcasm."

"I don't think Georgia was being sarcastic."

"I didn't mean Georgia."

"Neither did I."

And she wanted too much to believe him. "Let's see if you're still calling me *pretty lady* when I beat you to the bottom of the first run."

He tipped his head to the side. "It's all right to accept a compliment, Danni."

No. It wasn't. It wasn't all right to accept or believe in Adam's compliments. It wasn't all right to have this conversation with him. "Frightened of losing? Is that why you're being nice? So I'll go easy on you in return?"

He sighed. "Come on then. Show me what you've got."

It was late afternoon before they got back to Blake's chalet. They'd intended to return at noon. But the conditions on the slopes had been perfect. As they'd skied they'd slipped into the easy camaraderie they'd once had—at times teasing, at times earnest, always effortless. For the second part of the afternoon, when they should have been packed and departing the chalet, each time they'd made it to the bottom of a run, they'd looked at each other and one or the other of them had suggested, *one more*.

Technically Adam was a better skier than she was, a joy to watch as he swerved and swooped effortlessly down the runs, but while she couldn't quite match him in sheer skill and grace she made up for it in determination and what he'd laughingly called recklessness as she'd skidded to a stop mere inches from him at the bottom of a run.

For the afternoon, she'd allowed herself to forget who he really was, helped by the fact that if they recognized him nobody on the ski field called attention to who he was. So, it was a day without cameras or protocol or excessive politeness and deferential or preferential treatment. He'd waited in line with her at the small cafeteria, his hat low on his forehead and his glasses on, and sat outside at the picnic table where they'd sipped their hot drinks and eaten pizza before taking to the slopes again.

"We'll head back tomorrow morning," he said as they approached Blake's chalet.

She questioned him with a look but he gave no explanation. He never did. Not to her and, she was guessing, seldom to anyone. Their plan, when they'd stretched out their time on the slopes, had been to head back straight away once they were finished. She didn't want to ask whether he now wanted to stay because he wanted the day—with her—to continue. Like the day at Disneyland she'd once had as a kid, a day that she couldn't bear to end. But perhaps he was just tired and didn't feel like the drive, or perhaps he didn't want her driving after a day's skiing. Assuming they were ignoring the whole *you're fired* thing and that he would let her drive anyway. Always with Adam there were so many questions in her head because he let no one see what was going on in *his* head.

And the weak part of her that she'd denied for so long was just grateful that she would get to spend more time with him. Every minute delighting her. She wasn't going to question that. Not yet.

They stepped inside and stowed their gear in the drying room. But with the divestment of their outer layers, Adam seemed to put on an invisible layer of reserve, something that had been blessedly missing all day. He'd put it on as she'd taken off her jacket, and it became even more noticeable as she passed by him to exit the drying room. He backed almost imperceptibly away from her.

They walked silently to the living room.

Blake welcomed them with his customary verbose good humor, insisting that he'd have mulled wine ready for them in front of the fire as soon as they'd—and he used his fingers as quotation marks—freshened up.

So she showered and thought of Adam. Thought of the deep pleasure she'd found just being with him today. She'd sat on the chairlift with him, the hum of the wheel on the cable the only sound interrupting the deep quiet that was peculiar to snow. Sometimes they'd talked on the chairs, and sometimes they'd just sat. Both ways were easy. Both were blissful.

She was a fool. And she didn't know how to stop it.

She'd had relationships before, but they'd been mutual. And clear. Superficial and uncomplicated. Nothing like this.

This one-sided wanting was so much harder to deal with, so much harder to hide. She knew he did what he thought was best for her—but he had no idea. His definition of *best* and hers were poles apart.

He was passing her door when she left her room, self-conscious in a dress and heels.

Adam, as always, looked totally at ease. A soft black cashmere sweater stretched across his shoulders and hinted at the definition of his chest. He held out his arm for her, as though it was the most natural thing in the world.

And maybe for him it was. Doubtless he had held out his arm to women to escort them to dinner almost every night. But for her, just sliding her hand onto his forearm filled her with new sensations. Made her blood rush faster. It made no sense. They'd spent the whole day together. And she'd thought she'd put yesterday's insanity behind her. They'd been close the whole day. And though she'd had wayward thoughts, they hadn't had the intensity that gripped her now. She'd been able, so long as she wasn't looking at his lips, to put their kisses from her mind and not crave more.

But they'd also had on layers and layers of clothes. And she was acutely aware that she'd never touched him before in this supposedly neutral fashion, not since she was a kid when touch meant nothing except friendship, when touch didn't light fires of connection and possibility within her.

Resting her palm on the softness of his sweater, feeling the strength and warmth beneath it, well, it did bad, bad things to her. Made her think bad, bad thoughts. She wanted to lean in, inhale more deeply of his scent, the scent of freshly showered male. And she wanted his lips on hers, and his hands on her. She wanted to know so much more about him than he let her see.

What she needed, on the other hand, was to get farther away from him. So that her brain could start functioning properly again, so that she remembered who she was. And who he was. And that he was looking for a wife. One who met his criteria. Not a temporary fling with his temporary driver.

But, a little voice whispered, *that wouldn't be so bad, would it?*

His step slowed and she looked up to see his gaze on her. "What is it? Do I have toothpaste on my lip?" She ran her tongue around her lips to check. He shook his head and looked away.

"You look—" he cleared his throat "—nice. That's all."

"Nice?"

"Lame compliment, I know. But I don't think the right word to describe you exists. And in that dress…" His gaze swept over her; it didn't linger but there was something in it that warmed her. "Your legs…I scarcely knew you had any."

Danni laughed at his uncharacteristic awkwardness. She'd brought the simple black dress because it traveled well and still made her feel feminine, as did the glint of male appreciation in Adam's eyes. "I hope that's not supposed to be a better compliment." She tried to make light of the reaction to him that was sweeping through her.

His laughter was little more than a breath. But it warmed her further and compensated somewhat for the "nice." Not the best compliment she'd ever had. But coming from Adam, who doubtless had a wealth of sophisticated flattery at the tip of his tongue, it felt honest. And making him laugh always felt like a triumph.

The laughter was still there in his eyes as they held hers for a second.

He started walking again. Oh yes. She knew how he thought of her. As a kid. Almost a sister. That was why his "nice" had felt honest. Danni slid her hand from his arm on the pretext of adjusting her dress. And didn't put it back. *Nice.* It made her realize how much more she wanted from him.

Blake met them as they came down the stairs and insisted they sit in front of the fire while he brought the mulled wine. Adam tilted his head toward the chess set and when she nodded, he shifted it so that it sat between them.

He adjusted the pieces on his side of the board and looked up. "I owe you an apology and my thanks."

"An apology *and* thanks. Wow. That's a big day for you. I'm a little shocked."

"I'm serious, Danni."

"So am I."

He shook his head but a grin tugged at his lips. "Wait till you hear me tell you that you were right."

She slapped her hand to her chest and gasped. This was how she was supposed to behave—the teasing friend, not a woman whose mind was steaming down a one-way track that ended with his bones being jumped.

His grin widened briefly before disappearing. "I haven't had a day like that, as good as that, in…I don't know how long. I skied and forgot about almost everything. Forgot about brewing diplomatic crises and security concerns and upcoming engagements and speeches. Forgot about looking for—thinking of the future." Had he been going to say looking for a wife? "And I owe you for that. You made a good decision when you brought me here."

"Thank you."

"Nobody else would have seen that or done that."

"Because they're all too scared of you."

"Scared?" He sat back in his chair, his brows drawn together. "No they're not."

"In awe, might be a better word. Though I fail to see why." He was just a man doing his job. His job happened to be fairly high profile. But it was still just a job. And a demanding one that he needed time out from occasionally. Who was she kidding? Even she felt the awe occasionally. But in her case it was because of who he was, not what he was.

"I can live with awe," he said with a faint smile.

"It's not good for you. You'll lose touch with reality. You'll get a big head."

"A big head?"

Big Head was what she used to call him when he got all superior on her when she was younger.

Now he was laughing at her. Not out loud. But inside. She just knew it. And she felt her lips twitch in response.

"Thankfully I have you to keep me humble."

And scarily, she wanted to do far more than keep him humble. Things she wasn't supposed to want to do to a prince. It was there somewhere deep inside her, a humming attraction to him. Stronger when she was closest but always there. And she didn't know how to make it go away.

"I needed today. So thank you."

He'd needed today. He'd needed the time out. But he didn't need her. She bit her lip. She shouldn't want him to need her. But wanting her, just a little, wasn't she allowed to want that?

"What about you?"

"Me?"

"You enjoyed today?"

"Yes." Way too much.

"You seem thoughtful."

"I'm fine," she said a little too brightly. "Tired. In a good way. And hungry." In a bad way.

It had happened again. Since coming back here, the ease she'd felt with him had turned to dis-ease. The stiffness and politeness that he used to keep people at a distance was creeping back.

"So, are we going to play?"

"Sure. Can't wait to whip your…"

"My?"

She loved it when he smiled like that, knowledge in his eyes. "Your fine royal ass."

"Have at it."

If only.

They'd scarcely started when Blake returned with their drinks. "Dinner will be ready in half an hour. And you'll be relieved to know that the chef finally turned up. And whatever it is he's cooking, it smells good."

They sat in front of the fire, the chess set between them. The game gave her something other than Adam to focus on. But it wasn't enough of a distraction to keep her from noticing his hands as he moved his pieces and wanting those hands on her, or the deep concentration on his face when she stole looks at him while his attention was focused on the board, and wanting it focused on her.

She was contemplating the curve of his ear when he suddenly shifted his gaze to catch her studying him. His dark eyes trapped and held hers. "Your move," he said slowly.

If it was truly her move, she'd leave her seat and trace the shape of his ear, maybe run her fingers through his hair or over his shoulders, and definitely, definitely kiss his lips, seeking the taste of him, needing to feel that softness, to inhale something of him.

They were both leaning forward over the board. His face was close and she was trapped by the depths in his eyes.

Desire. It bloomed within her. And she recognized its match in the darkening of Adam's eyes. She tried to look away. Tried and failed. And she couldn't say for certain which of them closed that small distance. She'd thought so hard about it that maybe it was her. But it didn't matter because his lips were on hers. She closed her eyes and savored the onslaught of sensation. His lips, firm yet soft, the taste of cinnamon from the mulled wine, and his encompassing warmth. She gave herself over to the kiss. Let the sensations wash through her, claim her. She felt his hand at the back of her head, his fingers threading through her hair.

Unlike their earlier desperate kisses this was achingly tender.

Eight

"Dinner's ready." They broke apart at the sound of Blake's voice. "Oh, sh—sorry. I didn't mean to interrupt."

"You weren't interrupting," Adam said.

"Looked like I was, to me. Dinner can wait if you like."

"No." Adam who was never outwardly fazed by anything spoke almost curtly. He took a breath. "We're ready now," he said a little less abruptly.

"This way. If you're sure." Blake looked from Adam to Danni.

"We're sure," Adam said.

He led them to the dining room where it would be just the two of them with candles on the table between them and soft music playing from unseen speakers. Danni, whose biggest problem was usually saying all the wrong things, could think of nothing at all to say.

They focused on their appetizers, though neither of them ate much. Finally Adam set his fork down. "I'm sorry."

And there it was, his apology, an attempt to let her down gently, to take the blame and then reassert the proper distance between them.

"Don't be," she said warily. "It's me who's sorry."

"I shouldn't have kissed you then and I shouldn't have kissed you yesterday. I can't seem to help it. But it won't happen again."

She should say nothing, but instead, "Why not?" slipped from her lips.

His eyes widened. "I don't want to ruin or lose what we have and I won't take advantage of you."

"We don't have anything to ruin or lose." Danni's fork clanged against her plate.

"Yes we do. I trust you and I value you and I like you."

Like. That was at least as bad as *nice.*

"The last thing in the world I want is to do anything to change that."

"You're too late. It's already changed."

"How do we change it back?"

"We don't. We can't. And I don't want to. And it wasn't you who kissed me just then, it was me who kissed you. So you have no right to apologize for it. Ever since we kissed yesterday—"

"We shouldn't have."

"Since before we kissed, if I'm going to be honest." She pushed on before he could stop her. "I've thought of you differently."

"We can go back to how we were."

"I don't want to."

Adam looked stricken.

"I want to go forward."

"Forward?"

"I want to see where these new feelings go. I want you to kiss me and to touch me. All over. And I want to be able to kiss you, and to touch you. All over. And I want more than that, too." She waited, her heart pounding. Why, why, could she never keep her mouth closed?

Sorrow and a shadow of horror clouded his face. "We can't, Danni."

She'd known he didn't want to think of her that way. If she'd just kept her mouth shut, she could also have kept her dignity. "I'm sorry." Heat swept across her face as she picked up her fork and stabbed at a mushroom.

"It's not that I don't want to."

She looked up. His dark eyes were troubled. "At least be honest. Making up excuses would be worse than anything. A simple 'I'm just not attracted to you' will do nicely."

"I'm more attracted to you than I can stand. I kept skiing today—past when we should have stopped and gone home—just because I wanted to prolong being with you. Just being with you. Do you have any idea how extraordinary that is? I'm happiest on my own. Or at least I thought I was. But I've discovered that's not true. I'm happier when I'm with you. I can't stop thinking about you, but…"

There had to be a *but*, because for a while her heart had hoped and soared.

"I'm not going to do anything about it."

"Why not?"

"Because I'm supposed to be looking for a woman I can marry. A woman who can stand at my side and be my princess when I take my father's place."

"And I'm not that woman?" She was the opposite of what he was looking for. She knew it, she'd always known it, so it shouldn't hurt.

"Do you want to be?"

She almost said yes, till she thought about it. Danni laughed. "No. I can't think of anything worse." Except for the part where she would get to be with him in private.

"That's why I'm not going to do anything about it."

"Because there's no future in it."

He nodded.

"What about the present?"

"It wouldn't be right. It wouldn't be fair to you."

"Who are you to decide what's fair to me?"

"I'm not having this conversation with you."

"Do you see this appetizer we're eating?"

"Yes."

"It's not dinner. It's not the main event. It'd never fill you up, but it's very nice. So just because you're looking to start dating seriously so that you can find your perfect woman doesn't mean that while we're both here we can't…" She shrugged then took a deep breath. *Don't do it,* a voice of warning cried in her head. "I want to make love with you."

He shook his head. And in his eyes was hardness. And pity. "We can't. It wouldn't be right."

She'd just propositioned him, something she'd never done to any man. And been turned down.

And still she wanted him.

* * *

In her bedroom she changed into her pajamas—drawstring pants and a camisole—and sat on the big, empty, four-poster bed. She had no fantasies of a four-poster bed, only fantasies of Adam. So real she could taste them, feel them, so real they beat inside her chest.

Senses alert, she listened to the faint precise sounds coming through the wall of Adam getting ready for bed. The bathroom door opening and shutting, taps running.

He was attracted to her. He'd said that much—the admission wrung regretfully out of him.

But he wasn't going to do anything about it. That regret was hers.

Because it wouldn't be right or fair to her. Was the regret, the loss of something not known, never to be known, fair? Was sitting in here alone and needing, fair? He would do nothing about that injustice.

But could she?

A sliver of light peeped beneath the adjoining door. Was he thinking about her? Or had he put her from his mind? He was good at that. Deal with the issue at hand then move on to the next, letting no overlap complicate one or the other. He could be in there reading or working, totally focused.

But he'd said he was attracted to her. More than he could stand. And Adam was not a man to use words lightly.

She crossed to the door and put her ear to it but heard nothing. She touched her fingers to its hard, unrevealing, uninviting surface.

He'd already admitted that her going against his stated wishes and bringing him here had been a good decision. She could…seduce him. She swallowed a laugh that would have been close to hysterical.

Steeling herself, knowing that some regrets were bigger than others and some opportunities could never be recovered, she touched the handle. The beating of her heart precluded hearing anything else.

So few things in life scared her, but this…this terrified her. She deepened her breath till her fingers ceased their shaking.

She'd already made a fool of herself. She had nothing further to lose. Slowly, she turned the handle, holding her breath against the possibility that he'd locked the door from his side, and on her exhale swung the door silently open.

He sat at the small desk, his back to her and his laptop open in front of him but his head held in his hands. Trying to work? But not.

Drawn to him, to that broad back, that bent head, Danni crossed the thickly carpeted room.

Adam didn't move.

She stood behind him. His laptop had switched to its screen saver.

He straightened and held himself still, as though listening. She just had to touch him, one hand to the closest forbidding shoulder but her heart beat so hard she could scarcely move.

"No."

The single abrupt word was fierce. Sighing heavily, he rested his fingers on the keyboard and began slowly to type. A document with graphs and tables sprang to life on the screen.

That *no* was a message for her. What was she doing? She was no seductress. She was wearing her pajamas!

She didn't even own anything that could claim to be a negligee. He'd already turned her down. How much rejection did she want? Panic gripped her. She took a step backward, held still and then took another step. She backed halfway across the room on unsteady legs then turned. And she had her fingers on the edge of the door when his hand landed on her right shoulder and the shock waves reverberated through her.

"What are you doing?" His deep voice held both the question and his reluctant awareness of what her answer had to be. Given her earlier admission there could be no other.

"Nothing." She didn't turn to face him. She couldn't. Her heart thudded in her chest. Run. Run. Run. But she couldn't do that, either.

He stepped in closer. She could feel him behind her, surrounding her without touching her, except for that one touch, a heavy hand tight on her shoulder. Its grip invincible.

"Why are you in here?" His breath feathered across her neck sending warm shivers through her with the gently spoken words. Tension, beyond anything she'd known, seized her. A combination of wanting and anticipation and cowardice and fear.

He had to ask? As if her presence here wasn't obvious. She didn't doubt that women had tried to seduce him before. She was certain, however, that he'd never had to ask what they were doing. "I was going to burgle your room." Between that and seduction, burglary was surely the lesser sin.

"What were you going to take?" he asked quietly.

"Your innocence." She'd thought about making it a joke but her words came out a whisper.

His hand on her shoulder tightened and he pulled her back against him. She felt laughter reverberating through him. Okay. So maybe it had sounded like a joke. Apparently a really funny one.

But the silent laughter stilled. "My innocence is long gone, Danni," he said, utter seriousness in his quiet voice. "It's only when I'm with you that I even remember I had any."

She waited. His fingers tightened where his hand still rested on her shoulder. His breath still feathered across her neck though his breathing was shorter. And though the beat of her heart still commanded her to run, his hand and her recalcitrant feet and perhaps that whisper of breath kept her immobile.

"Maybe we should just forget I came in here."

"It's not going to be that easy."

"Nothing ever is with you."

"Why?" His other hand came to rest on her left shoulder.

"Because you never let anything just be easy. You're always analyzing life like it's a chess game."

From the floor below them came a crash and the rumble of Blake's voice.

Adam's hands slid lower till they curved around her arms, his touch gentle but unbreakable. "I meant," he said, and she imagined his smile, "why were you trying to seduce me?"

"How many reasons could there be?"

"More than you could imagine," he said quietly.

"Well apparently I don't have a very good imagination. Because as far as I can see there would only be one reason I would try to seduce you."

"Danni. Go. While you can." He moved. Closer still.

So that she felt the press of him against her back. His hands slid lower still until they wrapped around hers, holding her in direct contradiction to his words. His cheek was beside hers.

She closed her eyes and leaned against him, over-whelmed by him. His nearness, his warmth, his scent enveloped her.

Movement again, and then the gentle press of his lips against her neck. Need blossomed. Drenched her. Stole strength from her limbs so that she melted back against him, her head falling to one side to give him greater access to her neck because she needed this kiss. His kiss.

This moment of weakness might be all she would get from him. So even as the desire and delight engulfed her, she tried to catalogue the sensations. But the strength of them made cataloguing impossible.

He just was. And his touch did what it did. And called to something in her that was beyond reason.

And while his lips and touch worked magic on her, magic so powerful it needed access to no more than the bare skin of her neck, his hands moved again, sliding from her hands to her waist, sliding beneath her top. Skin to skin. His heat seared her so that her breath shuddered in her chest. She backed more firmly against him.

Hands and lips stilled.

Please don't let him stop.

She leaned farther back, trying to meld herself with him so that he couldn't let her go, couldn't push her away. And she felt the evidence of his need, heard it in the ragged hitch to his breath.

"Danni."

She heard too much in his voice. Regret and blame and apology. His hands started to slip away. He would ignore need and go with his idea of right. She gripped his wrists and his hands stilled. She guided them upward, trailing over waist and ribs till she led them where she wanted to feel them, covering her breasts. He groaned against her neck and his thumbs brushed over hardened nipples.

Her gasp matched his groan as need streaked through her, hot and fierce.

He dropped his hands and as she was about to cry out in protest he turned her around.

And kissed her.

Properly. Finally. The kiss she'd been waiting for all her life. There was no anger or regret this time. No sweet gentleness. There was only need. His lips against hers. His tongue dancing with and teasing hers, clamoring to learn her and please her. His arms wound tightly around her and his body pressed against her.

She returned his kiss. Greedily. She had wanted this for so long even while she'd denied that wanting. She'd imagined it, dreamed of it.

And it was everything that she'd imagined and dreamed only better and so much more.

And now that she was facing him, she too could touch. Lifting her hands to his face, she traced his cheekbones, his jaw, felt the rasp of beard against her palms. She slid her fingers through his hair to delight in its dark silk. But she wanted more, too. As they kissed she found the buttons of his shirt, fumbled them undone so that she could touch the warm hard planes of his abdomen, the contours of his chest, the strength of his back.

She was torn between the delight of slow exploration, the need to learn and treasure every contour, and the ravenous need to feel all of him, all at once, to fill her hands with him. She'd waited so long for this impossible reality and knew a fear that it might all vanish. It felt so much like magic, being held by him, kissed by him, that surely it could disappear as quickly as it had appeared, like a mirage in the desert.

Just as she'd feared, his hands came up, framed her face and he pulled back, breaking the kiss, ending the beauty.

He studied her and she tried to read his thoughts in his eyes. She saw turmoil and anguish. But she saw desire also. Deep, aching desire. It was there in his darkened eyes, in his parted lips and ragged breathing.

"It's not right," he whispered.

"It's very, very right," she whispered back.

And then he was kissing her again.

His attempt at restraint demolished, she could have cried in triumph.

He dropped his hands and wrapped his arms around her and carried her through the door to her bed. He set her on the floor. Torment clouded his eyes. His hands gripped her arms, their hold almost fierce. "Don't fight it, Adam. Just please tell me you have condoms."

A smile flashed across his face and he closed his eyes. "I give in. I'll be damned for it, but I give in." Relief weakened her. He was back from his bathroom within seconds and with slow wonder he peeled her camisole over her head and her pants down her legs. She helped him shed his clothes and they knelt facing each other on the bed. She helped sheath him and then Danni climbed onto his knees straddling him so that she could touch his face, trail her fingers along his nose, his jaw, over his lips. She'd wanted to touch him so badly for so long now, had done it countless times in her imagination. And the reality was everything she'd imagined and more. The hardness of muscle and bone, the silk of skin, the rasp of hair.

"Do you have any idea," he said, "how badly I want you?"

She bit her lip as she looped her hands behind his head. "I think I might." She shared that same need.

His hands rose to her breasts and a shudder rippled through her as his thumbs teased her nipples. She arched into his touch and he replaced his hands with his mouth, kissing each breast in turn, pleasuring her with lips and teeth and tongue while his hand roved, cupped her bottom and pulled her closer still so that his erection pressed against her.

He moved abruptly, swept her off him so that she was lying down and he was over her. "You are so perfect," he said, shaking his head and settling himself between her legs.

She wrapped her legs around his back. "Enough with the talking." She lifted her hips so that she felt him at her entrance. His passionate gaze locked with hers as he slid into her, stretching her, filling her as she'd ached for him to. Her body welcomed him. He stopped there, then slowly pulled out before filling her again, the pleasure exquisite. They moved together, perfectly in tune. The bliss built until it was almost unbearable. Sounds escaped her, cries of delight and need. Their rhythm built, became fiercer yet, unstoppable, till he was driving into her and she was meeting each thrust, taking him deeper still till the pleasure raging through her couldn't be contained and her orgasm ripped through her, shattering her. Adam surged against her, crying her name.

They lay, chests heaving, foreheads touching. As their breathing calmed he rolled off her but kept her in his arms. She laid her head on his shoulder, sated and dreamy.

Sanity slowly returned.

She felt and heard Adam take a breath. "Don't say anything."

"Not even, wow."

Danni laughed and he pulled her closer to him.

Adam woke and watched Danni sleeping, bathed in soft morning light. He could scarcely remember seeing her still before. Completely relaxed. Even when they played chess and she took her time thinking before making a move there was a contained restlessness to her as though she was ever ready to leap from her chair. It showed itself in the subtle tapping of her fingers or her toes.

He smiled now. She didn't share a bed well. She lay at an angle across the big bed. One arm was flung up above her head, her fingers curling gently. The pale skin of her arm looked so soft, vulnerable almost. Her eyes, usually flashing fire, were closed. Eyelashes kissed her cheeks.

She stirred and rolled. And the sheet he'd pulled up over her as she slept shifted. So beautiful. She took his breath away. Pale and lithe. More petite than he'd re-alized—again he blamed that restless energy that ra-diated for her, always making her seem…more. More than the sum of her parts. More alive than anyone else he knew. Brimming with vitality and humor.

The edge of the sheet lay across her chest, dipping low but not low enough to reveal her pert perfect breasts.

So feminine. He'd been willfully blind to that about her before. He'd focused over the years on how much of a tomboy she was, how she was his friend, at times almost a sister, to help him avoid focusing on the obvious. Danni was gorgeous. Passion personified. Nothing sultry, just an electric sensuality that called to him, like no one else.

Called to him? Like no one else? The thought stopped him cold.

He couldn't entertain thoughts like that. She was Danni. He was a brief pit stop on the race that was her life. And he had a life to lead, too. Responsibilities to live up to.

He should get out of this bed, cross back to his own room and lock the door behind him. Too late, he realized that he suddenly stood on the precipice of something unknown and dangerous.

She opened her eyes and her lips curved into a smile. That's where the danger lay. Those eyes. Just looking into them pleased him. Her smile broadened, she shifted again, arched just a little. He took back his earlier thought. Sultry. There was no other word for it. He rolled toward her. Precipice be damned.

She traced a pattern across his chest with her fingertip. "You know, French is the language of love but you never spoke French to me while we were…"

Making love? Neither of them would want to call it

that. "Because I couldn't think straight in any language. I can try now if you like?"

She grinned and her eyes sparkled.

He caught her lazily circling finger. "I'll speak words to you that will light you on fire. Words you'll understand even though you don't speak French or Italian or German." He brought that finger to his lips and kissed it. "Croissant, Citroen." He found her next finger, kissed that also. "Schnitzel, Mercedes Benz." Her fingers weren't enough. He rolled on top of her, holding his weight from her, and loved the way she wriggled to accommodate him and the heat and anticipation in her gaze.

"Go on."

He brushed her hair back from her face and kissed her forehead. "Pizza, Ferrari."

"Ohh, I think I like Italian best. Give me more."

"Demanding wench."

She rocked her hips.

And he'd give her the world. "Tiramisu, Lamborghini."

"Take me I'm yours."

He touched his lips to hers, and conscious thought, in any language, evaporated.

Nine

Adam stood with Danni and Blake under the portico of the chalet. Satisfaction thrummed through him as smoothly as the idling of the Range Rover's engine.

One night and one morning of perfection, of love-making and laughter. They'd stolen that much for themselves. As he watched Danni talking easily with Blake, he realized it was the laughter that had surprised him. He'd never laughed so much with a woman before. But Danni teased and joked, taking nothing, least of all him, too seriously. She was a revelation.

He hadn't thought she could be right when she'd said a relationship should be fun. It was one of the many lessons he'd learned from her.

Living in the moment was part of her nature. She had refused to talk about the future, about anything other than right now. And it turned out that very little talking at all was necessary and that there were far better ways than skiing to capitalize on snow on the ground outside.

The sheer compulsive energy of her had drawn him in. She'd uncovered a part of himself he'd walled over and forgotten.

He watched her now. Some of that energy had dimmed. Their time of isolated perfection was over. They were heading back. For the first time he could remember he was resisting what lay ahead.

"I hope you've enjoyed your stay," Blake said as though he was reciting lines from a script. He probably was. Several times throughout their visit, he had consulted the little red notebook that contained his instructions. Even absent, Sabrina ran a tight ship.

"Very much," Danni answered.

Blake leaned a little closer. "I didn't say anything, because I didn't want you to know." He lowered his voice. "But you were my first ever guests. I'm relieved it was you two. I don't know too much about this lark and I'll admit I was worried. I didn't know how it would go if someone important had come to stay. Sabrina would have killed me if I did anything wrong or got too familiar with guests. Or talked too much." A sheepish smile spread across his face. He winked. "If you ever see her and she asks, tell her I didn't."

"You didn't," Adam said.

"Anyway, it was a good practice run for me. We're expecting a mayor next week. I won't say who because I'm not allowed to talk about guests, but at least I've got this under my belt as a warm-up. I'll still be nervous having a local dignitary but it won't be so bad."

"Rest easy. You were the perfect host."

Blake slapped him on the shoulder with surprising force. "Thanks, mate. That means a lot to me. Oh, hey, I forgot to get you to sign the guest book."

"It's okay," Danni said. "I signed it." She tossed and caught the car keys. She knew he watched the movement. Challenge lit her eyes. He let the challenge pass. The driving was important to her.

Like him, she'd been reluctant to leave their bed this morning. But once she had, she'd approached the things they'd needed to do efficiently but almost mechanically.

They'd been on the road a few minutes when he asked, "Whose name? In the guest book."

"Just mine. And my signature's almost indecipherable. Don't worry, there'll be nothing to link you here with me." She didn't sound like the Danni of the last few days. There was a new distance and formality to her voice, and a subtle tension about her shoulders. Was this how it was going to go? Had he ruined everything by giving into the overpowering need and making love with her?

"That wasn't what I was worried about."

"No? What were you worried about then?"

"Would you believe me if I said you?"

She sighed but there was a hint of laughter behind it and her shoulders eased. "Yes. I would." The glance she flicked in his direction was almost sorrowful.

The road unwound before them, a dark damp strip between blinding white snow and dark green pines. The GPS in the dash showed what lay ahead. But there was no road map for what came next for them. And as a man who lived by plans and goals and schedules, the uncertainty and the changes they would face bothered him.

He didn't know if she realized what they'd be up

against. "You're the one who has the most to lose if this becomes public knowledge," he said. Hers was the life that would be turned upside down, its quiet privacy obliterated. He didn't want that to be the legacy for her of their brief time together.

"It won't become public knowledge. It can't. It was just one weekend." She sounded blithely unconcerned with her own fate. "Only you and I know, and I'm not telling anyone. And if you can curb your tendency to run off at the mouth," she said with pure Danni sass, "we'll be fine. Blake knows we were there together, but he doesn't know who you are. And even if he did I don't think he'd tell. Not deliberately."

"And there's always Sabrina to keep him in line." Blake had showed him a photo of the absent Sabrina, a tiny, sweet-looking woman.

"Exactly," Danni agreed with a smile. "One snowbound weekend. We were allowed that much."

But the possibility of what they'd shared becoming public was only part of what was bothering him. The other part, the purely selfish part, was the prospect of losing her, and what they'd found, so soon after discovering it. He'd been closer to her this weekend than anyone else. Ever.

"You're saying that's it, that this is over between us?" That was supposed to be his line, but hearing it acknowledged by her made him want to fight it. He wasn't used to this kind of confusion. Usually the right thing to do was obvious, or at least felt right. But ending things with Danni, when they'd scarcely started, felt wrong in his heart at the same time as he knew in his mind it was right.

She flicked a worried glance at him. "Yes. It has to

be. You know that. We have no future. We go back to life as normal."

That was the trouble. He did know. And yet she'd turned him upside down and inside out until he couldn't think straight. Because of her, he might never think completely straight again. But what he did know was that what he used to consider normal would no longer be enough. "I'm not sure it's possible."

"We'll manage." She spoke fiercely.

Did she really believe that? They'd come together so quickly there had been no slow anticipatory buildup, no courtship. None of the romance Danni herself had once informed him women wanted. Didn't she deserve that?

"And I'm supposed to be okay with just using you for a one-night stand? You're okay with that?"

"Absolutely. And you have to be okay with me using you. It was probably wrong of me but…" She shrugged.

He shook his head. Her voice held a brittle note of falseness. "I don't know, Danni. Things have changed so quickly and so absolutely. I need time to think it through."

"No, you don't. I can see where you're going with this. You think you haven't done right by me. But you have. Very, very right."

He didn't like the sudden stubborn lift to her chin, the narrowing of her eyes.

"You'll forget about the weekend and move on." She kept her voice low and easy but he thought perhaps she had to fight for that calm. "We both will. You're being honorable. I know you don't like the thought of using anyone."

"I wasn't using you. You know I wouldn't." But had he?

"Then I guess I owe you an apology, because you wouldn't. Not intentionally. But I was using you."

"I don't believe you." He recognized the tough kid who always came up fighting in the woman beside him.

"Believe me. I thought it was mutual or I wouldn't have…"

Wouldn't have what? There had been no forethought in what had transpired between them, no stopping to consider consequences.

She swallowed. "So while your protest is sweet, it's not necessary."

He couldn't see beyond the bravado, couldn't fathom what was going on in her head. And he owed it to her to find out. Despite what she said, he did need to do right by her. It was imperative.

"Danni, we need to talk this through."

"No we don't." She looked fixedly ahead. He couldn't see her eyes, and he needed to have some idea what she really felt. Her eyes, so expressive, always gave her away. "Let's stop at that café. The one we stopped at on the way up."

"I don't think that's a good idea." And still she didn't so much as glance at him.

"If what we have is over—"

"It has to be." She made his "if" an absolute.

"Then we'll be going to go back to how it used to be between us?"

"Yes."

"So, I'll cease being your lover and go back to being a prince to you, nothing more?"

"It's for the best."

"In that case, stop at the café. It's an order. And if you really want to prove things can go back to how they were, you'll follow it."

Danni took a deep breath and consciously relaxed her shoulders and flexed her fingers before resettling them around the wheel. Adam would come to his senses soon. All she had to do was to *keep calm and carry on.* It was either that or panic and freak out. When the café came into view she slowed and pulled in to the parking lot. An obedient driver. Nothing more.

Inside, the scent of coffee filled the air and an open fire blazed in the hearth. Only a couple tables were occupied, but at first one table, and then the other, heads turned. Then each of those few people leaned in closer to their companions. And whispered.

She could have kicked herself. Getting away without Adam being recognized the first time they'd been here had been more luck than she should have hoped for. A second time was too much to ask.

But, she reminded herself, the first time they had nothing to hide, and this time needn't be any different. She was his driver. Taking him home from his weekend break. *Of fantastic sex,* a wicked, insidious voice whispered. No. She was Adam's driver for the weekend. Period. If she repeated it enough times she could almost believe it. He was a prince. She was returning him to the palace. To his life. She should have worn her uniform. Because although it made her stand out, it also made her invisible. People saw it and then dismissed her.

Without her uniform she worried that people might see the woman who had spent the weekend in bed making love with a prince. She felt so different, so sexually satisfied, it didn't seem possible that the difference wasn't obvious.

Adam's nod and smile took in the occupants and the staff, earned him smiles and gasps in return. Somehow—through years of practice most likely—he'd mastered the art of looking warm and approachable while at the same time discouraging anyone from testing that approachability. He stood at the same booth they'd occupied during their first visit and waited for her to sit.

Danni slid onto the dark leather seat. Adam sat beside her. Too close. Too intimate. She scooted around so that she sat opposite him. Like a driver might. No. Not a driver. A driver would never sit like this with a royal client. But perhaps a friend. She could live with friend.

They ordered drinks from an effusive waitress who looked as though she might almost curtsy. When she'd turned her back, Adam leaned in. "Just a few hours ago we were making love." He kept his voice low, so as not to be overheard but it made it even more seductive than normal.

Danni didn't need his reminder. It was too easy looking at him to remember all that they'd shared. But she couldn't think about them making love. And he couldn't be allowed to, either. Or at least he couldn't be allowed to talk about it.

Deep down she knew she couldn't be just friends with him. Not after they'd been so much more. So her pending grief would be for the loss of both a lover and a friend.

In the space of days, things had gone further and deeper than she should ever have let them. She should have run far and fast that first night she leaned into the car to wake him and met his gaze and felt that insistent tug of attraction, the kick of desire. She should have run before she realized how very much more lay behind it.

"I just want to know that we've thought through our options before we consign 'us' to an impossibility," he said.

"We don't have any options and there is no 'us.'"

"There are always options."

"Not always. Not this time." They couldn't have options. It ended now. She could have no part of his life. She'd remember this always as something magical. But that was all it could ever be. A memory.

She had to be ruthless with the naive unthinking part of her that craved options and possibilities, that wanted to dream of a future, no matter how short, that wanted to steal all the minutes and hours and days and nights they could. Regardless of right or wrong. Regardless of the consequences because in this case they wouldn't be hers alone.

Adam belonged to their country, he wasn't hers and he never would be.

She thought she saw a shadow of the sorrow besieging her in his eyes. Beneath the table his foot brushed against hers. A small point of contact, toe to toe, through leather. They weren't allowed even that much and yet she couldn't move her foot away.

If they weren't in a public place and he reached for her, she would too easily succumb. As it was, he rested one hand on the table near hers and she ached to hold it.

"The trouble is that I can't bear for this—" he ges-

tured between the two of them "—to end. And I don't
think you can either."

"We don't always get everything we want in life."

He sat back as the waitress approached with their
coffees but his gaze never left her face.

"Don't you see," Danni said once the waitress had
gone again. "It has ended. It ended when we walked out
of that chalet."

His frown deepened, as though he might argue. But
he knew who he was and what he owed his country and
his family. He was returning to a world of responsibilities. Responsibilities that included looking for a woman
to stand at his side as princess.

"I can't stand by while you search for the perfect
royal wife. I'm strong, Adam, but I'm not that strong.
Or that much of a masochist."

He jerked as though she'd slapped him. His hand
clenched into a fist on the table. "And I'm not that much
of a bastard. How could I look at another woman after
you?"

"You have to."

He sat up straighter. The silence stretched and
stretched, till finally he spoke quietly. "I'm stopping
my search for the perfect wife."

The bottom dropped out of Danni's world.

No. She wouldn't be responsible for her country's
prince postponing his search. She'd be reviled throughout the principality.

She stood, her legs far from steady. "Then you definitely don't need me."

Ten

The drive back to the palace lasted an eternity. Adam sat as silent and inscrutable as a sphinx next to her. She just wanted the trip to be over. She needed to get away from him, because being this close when she could no longer have him was torture.

She would drop him off and aides would come running with crises for him to negotiate. He would move on.

But when she finally saw the longed-for towering sandstone building, it was loss rather than relief that swamped her.

This was it. This was their goodbye.

She drove to the entrance to his wing. He turned to her as she pulled to a stop. "Have dinner with me tonight?"

"No. I'm going to spend this evening with Dad." She took a deep breath. "Adam, don't do this."

"So when I kiss you now you'll be kissing me good-bye?" His dark beautiful eyes were steady on her, drawing her inexorably toward him. Desperation for this one last kiss. It was the desperation that told her she couldn't allow even this kiss. Especially this kiss.

"No. Yes. I mean, I can't kiss you, but if I did I would be kissing you goodbye."

Rational thought disintegrated as he leaned closer. She caught his scent, saw his lips—lips she knew so well. Every cell in her body yearned for his touch. One kiss. One memory to take away. She wasn't strong enough to deny herself that.

"You want this, too," he said softly.

"No, I don't." She was inches from him and she knew everything about her contradicted his words.

He laughed, the sound low and rich. And more than anything she wanted those laughing lips on hers. She pulled back and looked straight ahead, anywhere rather than at Adam. Adam, whom she could never have again. "You should get out now. We both have things to do. Lives to get back to."

"I'm not getting out. Not until you kiss me."

"That's blackmail." She couldn't let him win. If he was going to be stubborn then she could be, too. She got out, striding round the car to open his door and hold it wide.

As he got out, she walked quickly to the rear of the car and removed his suitcase. She carried it to the recessed entrance to the palace. She turned and found him right there. He lifted his hands to frame her face.

Just that touch of his palms along her jaw rendered her immobile, stole her breath. Made her ache. Her lips parted with need for him. She felt the familiar insistent tugging low within her.

"Tell me you don't want me to kiss you, every bit as badly as I want to kiss you. If you tell me that, then I won't."

She fought for long seconds over her answer, drowning in his eyes, aching with the need to touch him. "I don't want you to kiss me."

He lowered his head and brushed his lips across hers.

"You said you wouldn't." The feebleness of her protest echoed the weakness of her willpower.

"You lied when you said you didn't want me to. So that made my lie okay, too. Tell me you don't want me to kiss you again."

His breath mingled with hers in the cool air. She swayed toward him, her body betraying her mind. "I don't."

"Liar." He kissed her again, this time the way she needed him to, his lips slanting over hers, tasting her deeply, and filling her with the taste of him. Her arms slid around him, pulling his body closer, holding him to her, and any last scraps of reason fled. She was lost to him, lost to the sensations. His warmth, his scent, the exquisite pressure of his lips on hers, the way his tongue teased.

Finally, at a nearby sound, they broke apart and he rested his forehead against hers. His thumbs stroked her jaw. "This is wrong." His words whispered across her lips.

She knew he had to see and admit it sooner or later. But still the admission, when she was blinded with the need stirred by his kiss, hurt. "I told you."

"I should be dropping you at your door, not the other way around."

"That's not how it works. I was the driver."

"No, you weren't. I fired you, remember. I was only letting you drive as a favor. I know how you like it. So get back in the car and I'll drive you to the gatehouse."

"No."

"Yes. Or we go inside." He glanced at the palace. "I have a big bed in there, Danni. And I can't stop thinking about having you in it. This is your last chance before I pick you up and carry you inside. Maybe then I'll have you worked out of my system and can let this be over."

Danni saw the calculation in his gaze and knew she had only seconds before he acted on his threat. She strode from him and got into the passenger seat, shutting the door behind her. If this was how he wanted to play it… If it made him feel better, gave him the illusion of control, she would do it.

He drove her to the gatehouse and cut the engine so that all was silent before he turned to her, his eyes darkening, soulful and sinful. "Kiss me again."

She wanted to do so very much more than just kiss him. He was some kind of sorcerer making her forget what was good for her, what was right. And she had to break his spell without giving him the chance to weave a new one.

She leaped out of the car, shut the door with hasty, choked words of thanks and goodbye and ran into the house.

"You're sure everything is all right?" Her father asked for the second time that evening as she looked into the fridge trying to decide what to cook for their dinner.

"Fine, Dad," she said as brightly as she could manage. But she was far from all right. Adam had said he was stopping his search and it was her fault. "I'm just a little tired. I'm looking forward to a quiet and early night." Her first night of getting used to not being with Adam. Given that they'd only had one night in each other's arms it shouldn't be that difficult. What was one night out of a lifetime? Even if that night had been blissful perfection. There was no reason for this awful weight pressing on her heart.

"Oh."

She didn't like the sound of that "oh" and looked at her father. "What's up?"

"I must have misheard him."

"Misheard who?"

"Adam."

A knock sounded at the front door.

"Dad? What's going on?"

"Adam called earlier. He said he was going to come around to see you."

Danni strode to the door, her father's voice catching up to her as she reached for the handle. "Is there something going on between you and Adam?"

Her fingers stilled and she turned back. "No, Dad. There's not." Not anymore. On one hand he'd think she was breaking ancient unwritten rules if there was something between them; on the other, there was probably nothing in the world her father would like better. It would be a dream come true for him.

But this was her life and she had to live it to best suit herself, not her father.

Danni pulled open the door and came face to face with the man she didn't want to see. And all the memories of what they'd shared and being with him came flooding back, swamping her. The oppressive weight lifted from her heart and it soared like a bird unexpectedly freed from captivity. She stared at his face and it reflected some of the same hunger she felt.

She'd missed him. Damn it.

She'd only been away from him for a couple hours and she'd missed him. It was so good just to look at him. And despite the fact that he was forcing her hand in coming here, there was a trace of uncertainty and need in his eyes as he watched and waited. She should have capitalized on it; instead, that uncertainty and need undid her.

"Adam." She meant to say his name without feeling. Instead her voice was filled with yearning.

She drank in the sight of him. A sight she had to deprive herself of. Soon. But not yet. She needed just a couple more seconds first. Time to imprint in her memory just how he looked—his eyes, his nose with that bump, his lips, his jaw. She had to clench her hands at her sides to keep from reaching for him.

From behind his back, he produced a bouquet of flowers.

"You shouldn't have." The gesture was romantic.

"You don't like them?"

She lifted the bouquet to her face and inhaled the fragrance. "They're beautiful. Nobody's ever given me flowers before."

He reached for her shoulders and pulled her toward him. His eyes searched her face.

She tried to be strong. Difficult when desire swept

through her, overwhelming good sense, overwhelming everything.

He pulled her closer still and waited. Leaving her anticipating. Wanting.

Finally it was she who gave in and closed the distance, needing the touch of his lips on hers.

He released her too soon from the kiss that should never have happened. His hands had traveled to loop around her waist and he kept them there, kept that bond between them.

She should pull away.

She stayed where she was.

On a soft sigh Adam kissed her again. This kiss was full of the promise of delight and pleasure. It was long blissful seconds before he lifted his head.

"I spent the entire meeting with the Spanish ambassador thinking of doing that."

"But we agreed," she protested. Too little, too late.

"We didn't agree to anything."

Danni laughed. A mix of exasperation and despair. Why did it have to be Adam? The one man above all others she could never have. The one whose whole existence was so far removed from hers. He needed a woman who was her opposite, cultured and sophisticated, diplomatic and beautiful. Someone who would make a good princess.

And she needed to forget about him.

But at this instant, cradled in his arms, she could only be grateful that he was making a liar out of her and taking what he—and she—wanted rather than what was right for him.

"Come out with me tonight. We need to talk."

"No. I have work in the morning. A press conference to prepare for later this week."

"Don't leave him standing out there, Danni. Ask him in." Her father's voice came from within the house.

"No." There was no strength, only panic, in her voice. She couldn't let him do this.

"Come and watch this, you two," her father called. "They've got coverage of the Brazil race."

Adam lifted an eyebrow. "Watching Formula One with your father, what harm could there be in that?"

"All sorts of harm."

A hint of a smile touched his lips. "Frightened of me, Danni?"

"No." Liar. She was terrified of what he'd done to her heart, of the havoc he could wreak.

"Good, then you won't mind."

"Why won't you take no for an answer?"

"It's a failing. Weren't you supposed to cure me of my flaws?" He looked over her shoulder. "Evening St. Claire."

Danni's heart sank. If her father was here, there would be no getting rid of Adam. "Evening, Adam. Are you two coming in or are you going to stand out there in the cold all night?"

Adam watched her and waited, appearing to leave the decision—now when it was too late—up to her.

"We're coming in," Danni said on a sigh. She had no strength to resist. Her earlier attempt had been a bluff—and he'd known it. There would be time enough for strength tomorrow. After just this one evening, in the company of her father. What harm could there be in it? A little voice in the recesses of her mind echoed her earlier answer—all sorts of harm. Because she wanted so desperately just to *be* with Adam—near him, able to watch and hear him, to laugh with him for one more evening.

Tomorrow she would leave. Go stay with a friend. Go somewhere Adam wouldn't follow her. She would force a clean break on herself.

"Have you eaten?" Adam asked as she put the flowers into a vase.

She shook her head.

"Takeout?" He pulled his phone from his pocket. "Is Chinese still your father's favorite?"

She nodded. Her acquiescence complete. She might as well just roll over and present her stomach for him to scratch. Oh, wait. She'd already done that.

He followed her to the living room. Her father sat in the armchair, leaving her and Adam the couch. They sat close, but not touching, which was its own kind of torture. As her father added his commentary to that of the announcers, Adam's hand, out of her father's line of sight, found hers and closed around it. And this touch was too much and not enough.

The three of them watched, intent, conversing only occasionally, shouting at the screen at times. And despite knowing that she shouldn't allow it, Danni found so much pleasure in sharing this with Adam and her father that it hurt, this taste of what could never be.

After they'd eaten, she made coffee, needing an excuse to get away, a chance to regroup, to grow a spine. But in the kitchen she stood at the counter and stared out into the night.

Adam came to stand behind her. His arms wrapped around her. "The times I spent here with you and your father were as close as I got to ordinary growing up and you have no idea how much they meant to me. I knew my father loved me but it was your father who spent time with me, who had no expectations. I've always been grateful."

"I liked how you were when you were here. You were so different from when you were with Rafe or the other kids. You were so serious, so remote, as though even with them you had to remember who you were."

"I must have been insufferable."

"We suffered you." She smiled, remembering those times. She'd seen the barriers he erected, they all had, but she'd seen the chinks and breaks in the invisible armor he cloaked himself with. She'd seen them when he'd been here, or when it had been just the two of them, and he'd thought she was too young to really understand what was going on, and too devoted to him to reveal the secrets he sometimes revealed to her. She'd reveled in her perceived status as his favorite. She wanted it still.

She stepped out from the shelter of his arms.

What if I fall in love with you? She wanted to scream the words, the real reason for her fear. Instead she locked them deep inside her. Because she knew the answer to that question. It would be a terrible, terrible thing.

Eleven

Something was off.

Danni had been coordinating the biannual press briefings since the start of the process of bringing a Grand Prix to San Philippe. The feel in the room today was different. And it wasn't just her and her confusion over her feelings for Adam and her sorrow over what could never be.

The last official press release two weeks ago, back when her life had been normal, had contained promising developments. But not promising enough to justify the crowd in the small room that usually had more empty chairs than full ones.

She caught an enquiring glance from Michael Lucas, the head of San Philippe motorsport, and gave a small shrug. As well as the usual motor racing commentators, and representatives from tourism, who expected a Grand Prix to have a major influence on visitor numbers, there were reporters and journalists she didn't recognize. There was also a new sense of energy and excitement in the room.

As she stood to the side of the stage, she reviewed her notes again, including the emails that had come in last night and this morning. Nothing surprising there. She could only be glad that, after a drop-off in interest over the last few months while proceedings slowed down in talks about safety and scheduling and disruption to residents, awareness appeared to be picking up again nicely.

She tried to keep her thoughts on task, tried not to think about Adam, who she had missed so desperately in her bed this last week. She'd ached for his presence, his scent, the weight of his body next to hers. Missed the way he made love to her.

The first thing she'd done at work the Monday after her ski weekend was to make arrangements to move forward her trips to other Grand Prix host countries. She was getting out of San Philippe. It was the only way.

The sound of Michael clearing his throat recalled her attention. The panel, including drivers, and manufacturers' representatives were all ready. Michael looked for her nod then began the conference with the latest updates, then opened the floor to questions.

He took a couple of questions about the race course then chose one of the journalists Danni didn't recognize to ask her question. Danni could see the woman's press accreditation but from this distance couldn't tell which publication she was with. But if interest in the

Grand Prix was spreading to mainstream media she could only be glad.

"I have a question for Ms. St. Claire."

All heads turned toward her. Danni hid her surprise, but suddenly she wasn't quite so glad. As she reached for the microphone the end panelist held out for her, she had a very bad feeling.

"Is it true that you're romantically involved with Prince Adam?"

Danni clamped shut the jaw that wanted to fall open. Not interest in a Grand Prix. Interest in a grand prize. A grand prince. Gossip about her and Adam.

She'd really thought they'd got away with it, a weekend of anonymity. But it had been naive to hope they might evade speculation and that their time together would be something she could treasure and keep to herself. Just one weekend. Did Adam not deserve that? Whether or not he deserved it, he wasn't going to get it.

Interest in the room picked up palpably. Journalists, presumably the ones who hadn't known already, sat up straighter. Initial surprise and disbelief turned quickly to curiosity. Danni glanced at Michael, who was frowning but whose head was tilted inquiringly, waiting for her to deny the accusation. Her breath caught in her throat. She looked back at the reporter. "That's not something we're here to talk about," she said with a brittle smile. She signaled for Michael to take the next question. They needed to divert the reporters' interest. A distraction like this one was the last thing she wanted.

But the journalist wasn't about to let it go at that. "How would you characterize your relationship with the prince?" She called out her question, not waiting to be asked.

Danni paused, needing to shut this down and move on. She was about to issue a categorical denial—after all what she and Adam had was over, it had to be—when she looked up and saw a solid, dark-suited man standing at the back of the room. Wrightson, one of the palace drivers. What was he doing here? He gave his close-cropped head the smallest of shakes.

No? No, what? Don't deny it? Do deny it?

Danni took a deep breath and looked back at the woman. "How would I characterize my relationship with the prince? To you, very carefully. And that's all I have to say on the subject."

A murmur of laughter spread through the room. The motorsport journalists were no more pleased about the presence of tabloid reporters than she had been. Imposters in their ranks. Though undoubtedly many if not all of them were scenting new angles for their stories, angles that might sell more papers or subscriptions or ad space on websites. They might not all like it but they knew what paid their wages. She just had to keep the focus where she wanted it. "Now let's move on. Robert?" Robert Dubrawski, a newscaster with a background in finance, would be wanting information on the economic impact of a Grand Prix.

Through a mix of firmness and humor, she kept the rest of the briefing relatively on track. And when the allotted time was up, she took a back exit from the room and into the side streets walking quickly, wanting to put distance between her and impending disaster.

She knew a quiet little restaurant in the old part of the city. She could get a corner table and figure out what was happening and what she needed to do about it. She was hurrying toward the restaurant when a sleek dark Jaguar pulled alongside her, slowing to a stop.

The window slid down to reveal Wrightson behind the wheel. "Prince Adam wondered if you could spare some time to meet with him?"

Only if Prince Adam could wind back time itself and stop this from happening. She was about to refuse when she heard her name called out. The reporter from the briefing and a photographer were running up the street toward her.

Danni hopped into the car.

The breaking of their story changed everything.

They had to come up with a joint strategy, an excuse for why they'd been seen together. And doubtless, if they needed it, Adam would have the very best PR advisers at his service.

She switched on her phone, found a message from Adam asking her to call him and another more recent message from the receptionist at work advising her not to come back after the briefing because photographers were swarming the building.

Danni didn't speak as the car rumbled over the cobbled streets, crossed an arching bridge and headed sedately for the palace. She did her best to tamp down the anticipation that seeing Adam inevitably stirred. Fifteen minutes later they drew up outside Adam's wing. Before the car had quite come to a stop, Danni opened her door and got out. As she looked around, unsure of what to do, the door to Adam's wing opened and he strode out.

And despite all her resolutions, her determination that everything had to be over between them and her annoyance that what should have been private had been made public, her heart leaped at the sight of him. So confident, so intense. The concern in his eyes for her.

He strode toward her and caught her shoulders. "You're okay?"

She nodded.

"I'm sorry about the press." Regret and anger tinged his voice. If the press had wind of their story, there were only two ways it could go. They'd revile her for stopping him from finding a suitable woman or they'd expect him to confirm it was serious with Danni.

He wouldn't accept either of those outcomes. He understood his duty.

"It's not your fault."

He pushed a lock of hair behind her ear. "Actually it is. It's because of me they're interested in you. I never wanted them to get to you." Along with the regret and anger she recognized resignation in his voice, his eyes.

He knew, finally, that what they'd shared had to be over.

Even with all her attempts to convince him of that simple truth, his acceptance of it opened up an emptiness inside her that filled with a great welling sorrow.

"As soon as my secretary told me there were pictures, I tried to get word to you. Your phone was off."

"I'd put it to voice mail."

"I know. So I sent Wrightson. I would have gone myself but…"

"Fuel to the fire. I get it. Thanks for trying though."

"I'd have stopped it if I could."

"I know. But you can't and so we need a strategy. Is it too late to say there was never anything between us?"

"They have photos of us skiing and photos of us

leaving the palace grounds together. The skiing ones have only just come to light. But combined with the others..."

"Can they be explained any other way?"

He lifted a shoulder. "They could be."

"Then let's—"

"It's best to be honest." He brushed his knuckles across her cheek. "At first you were labeled a mystery woman. Unfortunately, but not surprisingly, it didn't take them long to figure out who you were."

"No. It wouldn't have." She thought of the reporters' tenacious questions.

"I heard you handled the press well."

"I managed. I think. The questions caught me by surprise. I was about to deny any relationship when Wrightson shook his head."

"Like I said, it's best to stick to the truth. It always comes out eventually."

"If we have to stick to the truth," she said, "we tell them we had a weekend together but that it was a mistake."

"I don't make mistakes. And you definitely weren't one."

"Then we tell them that it...didn't work out."

"Seemed to me that it worked pretty well."

"It did." For that one isolated weekend.

"So have you come up with a way to handle the publicity?"

"I've spoken to the palace advisers."

"And?"

"I also spoke to my father and to Rafe."

"Oh." Of course it was inevitable that his father and brother would find out and have an opinion. She shouldn't be surprised or dismayed. "What did they say?" She held up her hand. "No, wait. Don't tell me. I know what they said." Adam had needed to hear their views, but she didn't. It was surely them who'd finally convinced Adam that there could be no relationship with her. She should be grateful for that. "What's the strategy."

"As unoriginal as it is, 'No comment' seems to be the preferred strategy. That combined with no further contact between us. When there's no fuel, the fire soon dies out."

His gaze searched her face and he shook his head. "I've missed you." He pulled her to him. Acting on pure conditioned response, she rose up for his kiss and welcomed the touch of his lips to hers.

How could this be over when he kissed her like that?

How could she walk away from him?

His kiss, as always, sent sensations spiraling through her, weakening her legs, trampling over rational thought. That was why she was having such trouble walking away from him, she thought with a half laugh—weak legs.

She'd been too long without him.

He was her addiction.

As her hands, of their own volition, slipped around his waist, he pulled her closer still. Enveloped her in his warmth. Warmth that turned rapidly to heat.

Once more, a voice whispered.

Once more before it was over.

"Can you do one thing for me?" she asked.

"I'd do anything for you."

"Make love to me once more." She would take this and then nothing more.

He pulled back. She read the hesitation in his eyes and then his capitulation. He caught her hand in his again and strode wordlessly for the palace. He hurried up to the second level, past the library and along a hallway hung with portraits. The next door they passed through led into a bedroom. Unmistakably masculine.

Her gaze took in the room. He hadn't been lying when he'd said he had a big bed. There'd be room to turn cartwheels across it. Or make love lying any which way across it. She could turn cartwheels but she'd much rather make love.

A lock clicked into place as Adam pushed the door shut behind him. For one long delirious second they looked at each other. Awareness and unbearable hunger hummed in the air between them. Then he tugged on the hand he still held and she went to him. With no thought of talking she reached for him, undoing buttons and belts and zips, finding her way inside his clothes, needing skin on skin contact, the male heat of him, her addiction needing to be fed. One last fix. This close she could breathe in the intoxicating scent that was his alone. The one that called every cell in her body to attention. And the touch of him, the warmth that spread through her, were enough to reassure her that satisfaction was close at hand. Her craving would be satisfied.

Her only consolation for her senseless weakness for him was that he seemed as desperate as she was—lost to the haze of desire. Tugging and pulling at her clothes, with none of his legendary finesse. He eased her back onto his bed and lay down over her.

All the world narrowed to this one moment, this one man. All her thoughts, every sensation was centered on him and what he gave her.

He rose up, his broad shoulders and corded neck straining. Ready for him, needing him, she arched against him. He accepted her body's plea and in one long stroke drove in deep and fast, filling her so that her "yes" came out as a low satisfied moan, mingling with a similar inarticulate sound from him.

So good.

He felt so good. So right. So perfect.

And then he was moving within her, slowly at first but she didn't want slow and he responded to her needs, driving in harder and deeper and she reached for his hips, clasping the bunching muscles, moving with his rhythm, pulling him still harder and deeper, her legs around his back. Because she needed this. She needed him.

They strove together, swirling into the same vortex of wanting, racing for a release that demanded completion. Sensation, like licks of fire, swept through her, curling her toes, setting her aflame for this, for him, carrying them to that other mindless place till sensation couldn't be contained and the power of it surged through them as it crested and shattered.

Leaving her shaken and spent.

He held her in his arms as their breathing slowed and minds and bodies adjusted to the fact that they were no longer one. Aftershocks rippled through her as sweat cooled on her skin.

"Funny," he said later as he pushed a lock of hair from her face. "Whenever I dreamed about making love to you here in this bed, I imagined it to be slow and exquisite. I thought we'd take hours."

The awareness of Adam losing his ever-present restraint with her, thrilled and humbled her. "At least you got the exquisite part right."

His arm tightened around her. "And maybe we could try…"

She didn't know where she would find the strength to walk away from him because she hadn't known, hadn't let herself believe, that they could be this good together. That she could want more than his body or to give him more than hers. That he could make such a deep impression on her heart.

No, not an impression, he owned it. All of it.

The heart in question sank with the dawning awareness.

Love.

She'd fallen in love with Adam.

He was like no other man she'd ever known. She loved his seriousness, his complexity, his kindness. She loved him and everything about him.

A man she couldn't have. The irony was that he was the one person she wanted to share the appalling realization with. The Adam who was her friend as well as her lover in whose arms she now lay. The Adam who understood her, who always had.

But she couldn't admit her love. All it would do would be to make him feel guilty. He'd never asked for her love. She'd been an interlude in his search for a wife.

Maybe she should just be grateful that they'd taken as much as they had. More than they should have been allowed.

It was hard to be grateful when her heart was breaking.

She sought the temporary solace of making love with him again.

A long time afterward, a long slow exquisite time afterward, she rolled out of his bed.

Love wasn't supposed to hurt like this.

She found strength along with her clothes.

It wasn't till she was dressed that she turned back to Adam to find him watching her. Those now serious eyes had been fierce with fire and passion. For her.

This was it. The end. They both recognized it.

She turned away from those beautiful brown eyes and crossed to the window. Seconds later she saw his reflection in the glass. He'd come to stand behind her. Outside, darkness was falling. Her life had once been so uncomplicated. She leaned her forehead on the window.

Fifteen minutes later they sat in a nondescript sedan belonging to the palace's head of security. "I did your one last thing. Will you do one for me? Will you let me show you something?" He'd asked and she'd agreed. How could she refuse him? They skirted the city, crossed the river and several blocks later turned into an industrial area on the outskirts of the city filled with warehouses and light manufacturing. "Where are we going?"

"You told me once there were rumors that I had a mystery woman."

"Yes. And you laughed."

"You'll see why soon. We're almost there."

At the entrance to a light industrial complex, he pressed a code into a keypad that opened an enormous gate. Inside, he drove slowly past a series of closed roller doors, finally stopping in front of one. He pressed a button on his key chain and one of the doors slowly rose. He looked at her. "I haven't shown this to anyone before."

"You don't have to show it to me now." She almost didn't want him to. She had no idea what was behind that door, only that it was deeply personal to him.

"I want to." He drove into the dim interior. Danni instantly recognized a workshop, tools neatly lining the walls, and saw straight away the shape of a low, covered car. They parked alongside it and the door closed behind them.

She looked from him to the covered car. "Why would you keep a car out here when you have all that space at the palace?"

"This is private. It's nothing to do with the palace or being a prince. It's my escape from both of those things. Through that door over there—" he pointed to a wall "—are stairs to the top level. I had it converted to an apartment, just a bedroom and a bathroom. It's utterly private."

He tilted his head toward the shrouded car. "Let me show her to you. My mystery woman." They approached the car and he peeled back the cover. Her first glimpse of gleaming wheel spokes confirmed what she'd suspected as soon as she'd seen the shape of the low-slung car. "Dad's Bugatti. You're the collector?" She looked from the car, its engine exposed, to him. "How is that possible?"

"Your father did so much for me for so many years. Especially after my mother died. I wanted to do something for him in return. I knew he was selling the car at least in part for your college fees and that he'd never accept outright financial help. So I bought it through an intermediary. Don't get me wrong, it wasn't truly altruistic, having the car to work on has given me peace and much pleasure over the years."

"Dad doesn't know?"

Adam shook his head. "I wanted to finish it and then give it back to him. It's nearly ready. I steal an hour here and there."

Danni touched his face—her fingertips to his beautiful strong jaw. "That's a lovely thing you're doing."

He opened the nearest door. "Hop in."

Danni let him hand her into the car. Into the driver's seat. He took shotgun. "Do you remember—" she began.

"Yes. And I'm embarrassed about it."

"You said a girl couldn't drive it. That girls weren't good drivers."

"Thanks for reminding me. Did I ever apologize for that?"

"Not as such. But you let me drive for you. I figured that meant something."

"It did. And if it will mean something to you now you can drive the Bugatti. The detailing isn't finished but it runs like a dream."

Half an hour later they were parked on top of a hill looking back over the lights of the city gleaming like diamonds strewn across the night. A full moon hung partially obscured in the sky.

"I could sit like this with you forever." Adam's low voice reached across the darkness between them.

Danni looked away and surreptitiously wiped a tear from her cheek. She tried to swallow the ache in her jaw.

"I hope you find a good man, Danni."

She turned to him. "Would you be insulted if I wished you success in your search for a suitable wife?"

"To my core."

"So, don't…"

"I won't." He reached for her hand, held it with a clasp more fierce than gentle. "But I want you to be happy."

"And I want the same for you."

He tipped his head back and closed his eyes. He opened them again and looked at her with that intensity that was unique to him. "You know that if I didn't love you as much as I do, I'd ask you to marry me."

"You love me?" The words reverberated within her, filling her with joy and sorrow, her greatest wish and her greatest fear.

"With all my heart. I don't know when or how it started. And I don't know how to stop. You can't possibly know how vital you are to me. But I couldn't ask you to share a life that would make you miserable. Rafe made me see that."

A silence stretched between them. He loved her. He loved her.

Finally, she spoke softly. "If I didn't love you as much as I do I'd accept."

"You love me?"

"With all my heart. And I do know how it started. It began when I was five and you got that book down from the shelf for me. And I don't know how to stop either, or believe that you can possibly know how vital *you* are to *me*. But I'm not what you need. I'd be a terrible royal wife."

His hand tightened on hers. "The constant glare of

publicity, the tedium of royal engagements. I couldn't bear to see your joy in life diminished."

She allowed another small silence, turning his words over in her head. "People cope," she said quietly. "I coped with the press today. But what about my lack of sophistication, my lack of diplomacy? I couldn't bear to discredit you."

He freed her hand, shifted his to caress her face. "There are far too many sophisticated and diplomatic people in royal circles. What I need in my life is vitality and plain speaking. Someone who's honest with me. Someone I can be with in the quiet moments. And I've been told I need to learn to have fun. To be more impulsive. I need a lot of work. I could use help with that."

She wanted so desperately to help him with that. "I meet none of your criteria for a royal wife."

"That's not quite true. You meet plenty of the criteria on that list. You're good with the press, you're good with children and you're beautiful beyond belief, but none of those matter anymore because I drew up a new list."

"A new list? When?"

"When you first tried to tell me that we were over. I thought it might be wise." He lowered his hand and pulled a folded and crumpled piece of paper from his pocket and passed it to her. "I didn't do too well with it. I couldn't come up with much."

Danni spread the paper out on the steering wheel. There was just enough light to make out that there were a few words on the paper but not enough to read them. "It's too dark. I can't read it."

"It says, 'Item One—she must be Danni.'" He blew out his breath. "And that's it."

The moon rose up from behind the clouds, shining enough light that she could make out her name on the paper. "You're right. It's not much of a list."

"It was the best I could do."

"I'd say you need help with it."

"I probably do."

"You should add to it that she must love you. Because if she loves you, whatever she has to give up will be less of a sacrifice than giving up on love."

"And I guess you'd tell me I should love her in return? With all my heart? And be willing to do whatever it takes to make her happy?"

"Absolutely."

"So that's three simple criteria." He turned in the seat and lifted his hands to her face. "She must be Danni, she must love me and I must love her in return? Will you help me find her and help me convince her to marry me, to never leave me?"

"Yes," she sighed. "But only if you kiss me now."

Epilogue

"Have I told you how beautiful you look tonight?" Adam stood and held out his hand to Danni.

"Yes." She put her hand in his, stood and walked to the dance floor with him, stepping gladly, gratefully into his arms.

They were the third couple to occupy the floor. The bridal couple, Rebecca and Logan, danced, eyes for only each other. Their wedding had been beautiful, full of pomp and splendor, but with human touches and laughter and most of all love.

Their love for each other had shone through every moment and every syllable of the service from the time Rebecca had taken her first step on the long walk up the cathedral's aisle.

Rebecca had looked amazing in her ivory silk and

lace gown and Logan had been visibly stunned as he watched her walk toward him.

Danni and Adam were among the very few who knew that beneath Rebecca's gown the first addition to their family already grew.

Rafe and Lexie danced now too, holding tight to each other. Their baby, Bonnie, had punctuated the service with her laughing gurgles, a delightful counterpoint to the beautiful solemnity of the occasion. Bonnie had stayed through the official luncheon but had been taken home by the nanny before this more intimate dinner and dance for a mere three hundred. But if they followed the pattern Danni had quickly become aware of, Rafe and Lexie would soon head home, too. Wanting to be with each other and their child had suddenly become a singular priority. The playboy prince had become a doting husband and father, completely besotted with the two women in his life.

At the head table, Prince Henri and Danni's father sat back in their chairs, sipping cognac and watching over proceedings with obvious fatherly pride.

Adam hadn't taken too long to bring his father round to the idea of their marrying. He'd had several meetings alone with him before bringing Danni to meet him officially. The main thing Prince Henri had wanted to be certain of was that they were resolute in their love for each other—because there would, he assured them, be trials. But once he was convinced of their love, he'd insightfully predicted that the country too would grow to love Danni. They would see her as just like them, an ordinary citizen, a commoner whom they could claim as one of their own and love. She would be the fairy tale come true.

And he'd been right. The press had quickly decided they were on Danni's side and made much of the work she'd done in bringing a Grand Prix to San Philippe. And they frequently pointed out how refreshing she would be for the royal family. Already it seemed that their prince, who they acknowledged could sometimes seem a little reserved, looked more relaxed and open. It helped that every photo they printed showed both Danni and Adam radiant with happiness.

Gradually, other couples joined the dance floor. So much had changed for Danni and Adam in the last month. They'd announced their engagement at Christmas. They'd considered waiting until after this wedding but speculation had been so intense that it seemed easiest to admit the truth, that yes they loved each other and wanted to marry.

Their wedding wouldn't be for another eight months. It was the soonest that it could be arranged given the pomp and ceremony that was apparently necessary, more even than there had been today. But, after all, it wasn't every day the heir apparent got married. The country wanted to celebrate, just as, after being robbed of a wedding by Rafe and Lexie eloping, they'd anticipated and then celebrated today's occasion.

Already a provisional guest list was being drawn up. Many of the names on it would be dictated by protocol and etiquette, with attention paid to international considerations. She and Adam were content to leave much of it to their aides, though they had made sure to insist that Blake be on it.

The only thing that really mattered to Danni was that she got to be with Adam. For the rest of their lives.

He danced with her, holding her closer than decorum suggested was proper, their bodies pressed together from shoulders to toes. Almost heaven, Danni thought as she swayed in his arms. Moving with him, being held by him. Every time she thought it couldn't get any better, it did.

"You look stunning in that dress." The dress in question had been made for her, a beaded evening gown, with simple flowing lines, in deepest purple.

"Thank you, but you know as soon as we get home I'll be kicking off these shoes and getting changed." She was gradually getting used to the formality of dress that was now often required of her, but she still liked her jeans best of all.

"You'll be getting out of the dress, do you mean? I'll be happy to help you with that." He pulled her closer still and spun her.

"So long as you're more help than you were when I was trying to put it on."

"The trouble is, as beautiful as it looks on you, it looks even better off you." He leaned down and whispered in her ear. "Though I guess you could keep the shoes on if you like."

Danni laughed. She couldn't believe she'd once accused him of lacking fun and spontaneity. In public he was seriousness personified. In private he was anything but. And she loved every facet of him.

* * * * *

PASSION

For a spicier, decidedly hotter read—
this is your destination for romance!

COMING NEXT MONTH
AVAILABLE JANUARY 10, 2012

#2131 TERMS OF ENGAGEMENT
Ann Major

#2132 SEX, LIES AND THE SOUTHERN BELLE
Dynasties: The Kincaids
Kathie DeNosky

#2133 THE NANNY BOMBSHELL
Billionaires and Babies
Michelle Celmer

#2134 A COWBOY COMES HOME
Colorado Cattle Barons
Barbara Dunlop

#2135 INTO HIS PRIVATE DOMAIN
The Men of Wolff Mountain
Janice Maynard

#2136 A SECRET BIRTHRIGHT
Olivia Gates

You can find more information on upcoming Harlequin® titles,
free excerpts and more at www.HarlequinInsideRomance.com.

HDCNM1211

REQUEST YOUR FREE BOOKS!
2 FREE NOVELS PLUS 2 FREE GIFTS!

Harlequin® *Desire*

ALWAYS POWERFUL, PASSIONATE AND PROVOCATIVE

YES! Please send me 2 FREE Harlequin Desire® novels and my 2 FREE gifts (gifts are worth about $10). After receiving them, if I don't wish to receive any more books, I can return the shipping statement marked "cancel." If I don't cancel, I will receive 6 brand-new novels every month and be billed just $4.30 per book in the U.S. or $4.99 per book in Canada. That's a saving of at least 14% off the cover price! It's quite a bargain! Shipping and handling is just 50¢ per book in the U.S. and 75¢ per book in Canada.* I understand that accepting the 2 free books and gifts places me under no obligation to buy anything. I can always return a shipment and cancel at any time. Even if I never buy another book, the two free books and gifts are mine to keep forever.

225/326 HDN FEF3

Name	(PLEASE PRINT)	
Address		Apt. #
City	State/Prov.	Zip/Postal Code
Signature (if under 18, a parent or guardian must sign)		

Mail to the **Reader Service:**
IN U.S.A.: P.O. Box 1867, Buffalo, NY 14240-1867
IN CANADA: P.O. Box 609, Fort Erie, Ontario L2A 5X3

Not valid for current subscribers to Harlequin Desire books.

Want to try two free books from another line?
Call 1-800-873-8635 or visit www.ReaderService.com.

* Terms and prices subject to change without notice. Prices do not include applicable taxes. Sales tax applicable in N.Y. Canadian residents will be charged applicable taxes. Offer not valid in Quebec. This offer is limited to one order per household. All orders subject to credit approval. Credit or debit balances in a customer's account(s) may be offset by any other outstanding balance owed by or to the customer. Please allow 4 to 6 weeks for delivery. Offer available while quantities last.

Your Privacy—The Reader Service is committed to protecting your privacy. Our Privacy Policy is available online at www.ReaderService.com or upon request from the Reader Service.

We make a portion of our mailing list available to reputable third parties that offer products we believe may interest you. If you prefer that we not exchange your name with third parties, or if you wish to clarify or modify your communication preferences, please visit us at www.ReaderService.com/consumerchoice or write to us at Reader Service Preference Service, P.O. Box 9062, Buffalo, NY 14269. Include your complete name and address.

HDES11B

Brittany Grayson survived a horrible ordeal at the hands of a serial killer known as The Professional... who's after her now?

Harlequin® Romantic Suspense presents a new installment in Carla Cassidy's reader-favorite miniseries,
LAWMEN OF BLACK ROCK.

Enjoy a sneak peek of
TOOL BELT DEFENDER.

Available January 2012
from Harlequin® Romantic Suspense.

"**B**rittany?" His voice was deep and pleasant and made her realize she'd been staring at him openmouthed through the screen door.

"Yes, I'm Brittany and you must be…" Her mind suddenly went blank.

"Alex. Alex Crawford, Chad's friend. You called him about a deck?"

As she unlocked the screen, she realized she wasn't quite ready yet to allow a stranger inside, especially a male stranger.

"Yes, I did. It's nice to meet you, Alex. Let's walk around back and I'll show you what I have in mind," she said. She frowned as she realized there was no car in her driveway. "Did you walk here?" she asked.

His eyes were a warm blue that stood out against his tanned face and was complemented by his slightly shaggy dark hair. "I live three doors up." He pointed up the street to the Walker home that had been on the market for a while.

"How long have you lived there?"

"I moved in about six weeks ago," he replied as they

walked around the side of the house.

That explained why she didn't know the Walkers had moved out and Mr. Hard Body had moved in. Six weeks ago she'd still been living at her brother Benjamin's house trying to heal from the trauma she'd lived through.

As they reached the backyard she motioned toward the broken brick patio just outside the back door. "What I'd like is a wooden deck big enough to hold a barbecue pit and an umbrella table and, of course, lots of people."

He nodded and pulled a tape measure from his tool belt. "An outdoor entertainment area," he said.

"Exactly," she replied and watched as he began to walk the site. The last thing Brittany had wanted to think about over the past eight months of her life was men. But looking at Alex Crawford definitely gave her a slight flutter of pure feminine pleasure.

Will Brittany be able to heal in the arms of Alex,
her hotter-than-sin handyman...or will a second
psychopath silence her forever? Find out in
TOOL BELT DEFENDER
Available January 2012
from Harlequin® Romantic Suspense
wherever books are sold.

SPECIAL EDITION

Life, Love and Family

Karen Templeton

introduces

The FORTUNES *of* TEXAS: Whirlwind Romance

When a tornado destroys Red Rock, Texas, Christina Hastings finds herself trapped in the rubble with telecommunications heir Scott Fortune. He's handsome, smart and everything Christina has learned to guard herself against. As they await rescue, an unlikely attraction forms between the two and Scott soon finds himself wanting to know about this mysterious beauty. But can he catch Christina before she runs away from her true feelings?

FORTUNE'S CINDERELLA

Available December 27th wherever books are sold!

www.Harlequin.com

SSE65643